"I don't regret meeting you, Rebecca. If there is anything I regret then it's that we didn't meet before."

Before Antonio.

The words hung between them, unspoken yet clear all the same. Becky felt her heart pound when she looked into his eyes and saw the expression they held. There was regret in them, but it was mingled with another emotion that made her body burn with a sudden, intense heat. To know that Felipe still wanted her that morning, as he had wanted her the previous night, made her feel as though the bottom had just dropped out of her world.

If he was longer her enemy then how much more difficult was it going to be to keep her secret from him?

JENNIFER TAYLOR lives in the northwest of England with her husband Bill. She had been writing Harlequin romances for some years, but when she discovered Harlequin Medical Romance novels, she was so captivated by these heartwarming stories that she set out to write them herself! When she is not writing or doing research for her latest book, Jennifer's hobbies include reading, traveling, walking her dog and retail therapy (shopping!). Jennifer claims all that bending and stretching to reach the shelves is the best exercise possible. She's always delighted to hear from readers, so visit her at www.jennifer-taylor.com.

HIS BROTHER'S SON

JENNIFER TAYLOR

MEDITERRANEAN DOCTORS

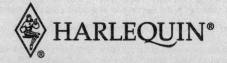

HARLEQUIN®

TORONTO • NEW YORK • LONDON
AMSTERDAM • PARIS • SYDNEY • HAMBURG
STOCKHOLM • ATHENS • TOKYO • MILAN • MADRID
PRAGUE • WARSAW • BUDAPEST • AUCKLAND

ISBN 0-373-82011-9

HIS BROTHER'S SON

First North American Publication 2002.

Copyright © 2002 by Jennifer Taylor.

www.eHarlequin.com

Printed in U.S.A.

CHAPTER ONE

IT STILL wasn't too late to change her mind. All she had to do was ask the taxi-driver to take her back to the airport. She might be able to catch an earlier flight back to London and...

And what? The situation hadn't changed. She was in exactly the same position as she had been in that morning when she'd set out to Mallorca. No matter how much the idea terrified her she had to accept that she needed Felipe Valdez's help.

'Señorita?'

Rebecca Williams started when the taxi-driver turned to her. She looked up in surprise, feeling her stomach churn with nerves when she realised they had stopped. Her grey eyes widened as she looked out of the window and got her first glimpse of the Clinica Valdez.

It was so much bigger than she'd expected. Maybe it was the word 'clinic' that had misled her because she'd never imagined it would be so imposing. As her gaze swept over the elegant, whitewashed building set in the midst of several acres of manicured lawns she could feel her heart racing.

Antonio had told her that his brother had founded the clinic two years previously, but she hadn't realised before exactly what an achievement that had been. Just raising the finance for such a venture must have needed a great deal of determination, plus a ruthless will to succeed. Added to what she already knew about Felipe Valdez, it wasn't encouraging.

Was he really the kind of man who would be prepared to help her financially without expecting something in return?

Becky bit her lip as a wave of panic threatened to engulf her. She could be making a big mistake...a *huge* mistake...if she went in there and asked to see Valdez when she had no idea how he would react to what she had to tell him.

5

Announcing that his brother had had a son would be bound to come as a shock to him. Then there were the circumstances surrounding Josh's birth.

Whilst Felipe Valdez might accept that his brother had been right to protect his unborn child, would he approve of her role in the baby's life? What if he decided to use his money and influence to take Josh away from her?

It might not be enough that she was Josh's legal guardian. The courts would need to take account of all sorts of issues if there was a battle for custody. She barely earned enough to meet their bills, and the fact that she had needed to return to full-time work at St Leonard's Hospital might also go against her. What chance would she really have of keeping the little boy when she wasn't his natural mother…?

'Señorita! Por favor!'

Becky jumped when the taxi driver spoke sharply to her. It was obvious that he was impatient for her to get out so that he could find another fare. She quickly pulled some money out of her bag and paid him, thinking that she may as well get out now that she was here.

She just needed a little more time to think everything through properly. She couldn't afford to make a mistake. She had to be sure that she was making the right decision—for Josh's sake.

Felipe Valdez sighed as he got up from his desk. He'd spent the best part of the morning dealing with paperwork. It was an aspect of his job which he particularly loathed but there was no way to avoid it.

As director of the Clinica Valdez, his say-so was needed before any decisions could be taken. Oh, he had some excellent people working for him, but he preferred to keep his finger very firmly on the pulse. He knew that his staff considered him to be something of a control freak, but they didn't understand. The Clinica Valdez was not only his greatest achievement—it was the main focus of his life. He had worked too hard and made too many sacrifices to take a chance on anything going wrong.

A frown drew his thick, black brows together because that thought had caused him more than a little pain. He tried not to think about the mistakes he had made in his life, but sometimes it wasn't easy to block them out. Now, as he looked out of the window at the sunlit grounds of the private hospital, he felt a familiar ache settle in his heart as he thought about his brother Antonio.

If he hadn't been so busy opening the clinic, he might have realised that something was wrong with Antonio. Maybe he would have been able to make his brother understand that he had to continue to receive proper medical care. Antonio should *never* have been allowed to leave hospital when he'd been so ill. With the right kind of treatment he could have lived for another six months at least.

Not that he blamed Antonio, of course. He had been too ill to realise what he'd been doing, too ill and too much under the influence of that woman. No, if anyone was to blame for Antonio's premature death, it was Rebecca Williams!

Felipe's mouth thinned. With his austerely handsome features he looked even more forbidding as he stared out of the window. He tried not to think about Rebecca Williams very often because it was pointless getting upset. However, sometimes he found himself wishing that he'd gone to see her in London after Antonio's funeral and told her exactly what he thought about her.

Only close family and friends had attended the service in Mallorca. Rebecca Williams certainly hadn't been invited so they'd never met. He had seen a photograph of her, however, and even though he'd torn it up he could still recall every detail, from the long blonde hair falling softly around her oval face to those huge grey eyes. She had looked like every man's vision of a ministering angel, but he knew how misleading appearances could be. Was it any wonder that poor Antonio had been deceived?

A woman suddenly walked along the path beneath his window and Felipe blinked. Just for a moment he felt his mind spin as he stared at her. Her blonde hair was caught up into a knot on the top of her head and her face was in profile, but there was something strangely familiar about her...

His heart began to pound as he turned and strode to the door. He wrenched it open, startling his secretary who had been about to knock. Felipe shook his head when she opened her mouth to speak.

'Later!' he ordered in a tone that brooked no argument.

He hurried into the corridor, taking the stairs two at a time as he raced down to the ground floor. There was a queue of people in Reception but he didn't pause as he made his way to the entrance. His heart was pounding, the blood drumming painfully in his ears, the need to check if he'd been right urging him on. If it *had* been Rebecca Williams walking past his window just now then, by God, he didn't intend to let her escape!

She was sitting on a bench outside the main doors. Felipe ground to a halt, feeling his breath coming in laboured spurts. There was something almost tragic about the way she sat there so still, so alone. When a wisp of pale blonde hair blew across her face, he was shocked when he saw how her hand trembled as she tucked it behind her ear.

He was suddenly overwhelmed by a feeling of compassion that stunned him because it was the last thing he'd expected to feel if they ever met. She looked so sad, so lonely, so deeply unhappy that his heart was immediately touched before he forced himself to remember who and what she was.

This was the woman who had hastened Antonio's death because of her own greed for his money. Did he really have any sympathy to spare for someone like her?

He must have made some small sound of disgust because she suddenly glanced round and he saw the colour drain from her face. She rose to her feet and he could see the tremor that passed through her slender body and was pleased. He had no idea why she had come to see him but it didn't really matter. It was enough that he would have the chance to tell her what he thought of her at last.

'You're Antonio's brother, aren't you?'

Her voice was low and surprisingly sweet. He frowned because it surprised him that he should have noticed a thing like that.

'I am Felipe Valdez,' he said harshly, and saw her flinch. He took a few quick steps and stopped in front of her, surprised once again when he realised how tiny she was. For some reason he'd imagined that she would be much taller and far less fragile-looking, so it threw him off balance for a moment to realise that the image he'd formed of her hadn't been wholly accurate.

'You probably don't know who I am,' she began in that low, sweet voice, but he curtly interrupted her, irritated that his mind should start running off at tangents at a time like this.

'You're Rebecca Williams. My brother's girlfriend, for want of a better description.' He smiled thinly when he saw her surprise. 'Antonio sent me a photograph of you. He said that he wanted me to see the most important person in his life.'

'I didn't know... He never told me...' Her grey eyes filled with tears and she turned away while she hunted a tissue out of her bag.

Felipe's hands clenched because the urge to touch her then was so very strong. It shocked him to the depths of his being that he should feel such a need to comfort her, shocked and angered him because wasn't it an indication of her power? If he could be manipulated like this, how much easier must it have been for her to persuade Antonio to do what she'd wanted?

The thought was just what he needed. Placing his hand under her elbow, he briskly steered her away from the main entrance, ignoring her murmured protest as he led her along the path until they reached a sheltered spot well away from any prying eyes. He had no idea what she wanted but he preferred to keep their dealings private if possible.

He had never spoken of his feelings about this woman to anyone, and certainly hadn't shared the contempt he felt for her with any of his colleagues. He preferred to keep his own counsel when something affected him deeply. Only once in his life had he ever opened his heart to anyone, and look how badly that had turned out.

He was surprised when that thought crossed his mind because it had been years since he'd thought about his engagement to Teresa and how it had ended. He had no time to dwell on it, however, as Rebecca Williams wrenched her arm out of his grasp. There was a touch of colour in her face and a glint in her grey eyes that told him she was angry about the way he'd behaved towards her, but she had forfeited her right to be treated with courtesy after what she had done to Antonio.

'I don't know what you think you're doing—' she began hotly, but he brusquely interrupted her once more.

'What precisely do you want, Miss Williams?' He smiled sardonically when she fell silent and stared warily at him. 'You must have had a reason for coming here, so why don't you tell me what it is? What is that wonderful phrase you use in England? Ah, yes, beating about the bush. I can see no point in us beating about the bush. *Sí?*'

'Who said that I wanted anything?' She walked a little way across the grass then turned to face him. 'I might have come here purely and simply because I wanted to meet you.'

'You might, but I don't think so.' Felipe folded his arms and studied her closely, knowing that all the contempt he felt must be clear to see in his sherry-brown eyes.

She was beautiful, all right, with that silky, pale hair, those delicate features, that air of innocence, but he wasn't fool enough to be taken in. Rebecca Williams was a cold-hearted, mercenary gold-digger, and it broke his heart to know that his brother had fallen into her clutches when he'd been at his most vulnerable.

Anger burned hotly inside him but he'd learned a long time ago how to use it to its best effect. He continued to study her, watching the play of emotions that crossed her face before her head suddenly bowed. When she spoke this time her voice echoed with a pain that sounded almost real—if he'd been foolish enough to believe that a woman like her was capable of any genuine emotions.

'You hate me, don't you? I can hear it in your voice, see it in your eyes.'

She suddenly looked up and Felipe felt his stomach clench when he saw the bewilderment in her beautiful grey eyes. 'Why? I don't understand why you should feel like that. I've never done anything to hurt you. We hadn't even met until today. So why do you…you *loathe* me like this?'

'Why do you think, Miss Williams? The answer isn't all that difficult, surely?'

He closed his mind to the swift stab of guilt that had speared through him. Rebecca Williams was a consummate actress. She must be if she'd managed to fool Antonio for all that time. How long had it been that she and his brother had lived together?

He was rather hazy about the details because it had been a while before Antonio had written to tell him the address where he was staying in England, and even then all he'd said in the letter had been that he'd met someone and that they were living together in London. Felipe hadn't heard from him again for many months, not until after Antonio had signed himself out of hospital after refusing further treatment. By the time that letter had reached him, his brother had been dead.

'Because of Antonio, you mean? But why? I don't understand. I never did anything to harm your brother. All I ever wanted was to help him!'

He pushed the memory to the back of his mind because he couldn't deal with it right then. Rebecca Williams was staring at him, and if he'd been gullible enough he might have believed that she really was as shocked as she was making herself out to be.

'Really? How touching.' He treated her to a contemptuous smile and saw her flinch. 'So you had Antonio's welfare at heart, did you?'

'Of course! I don't know why you need to ask me that. Everything I did was aimed purely and simply at making his life more…more bearable.'

Her voice broke and she looked away. Felipe's hands

clenched because he wasn't sure if he wanted to shake her or hug her at that moment. She'd sounded so sincere and yet how could he believe a word she said when he had indisputable evidence to the contrary?

It shocked him that he should feel this strange mixture of emotions when the situation was so clear cut. He knew what she'd done so maybe it was time he let her know that rather than allow the situation to turn into a complete farce.

'And the fact that you managed to greatly improve the quality of your own life was your reward for making my brother's last few weeks on this earth bearable? Is that what you are saying, Miss Williams?'

'I don't know what you mean…' she began, then suddenly stopped. He saw her take a deep breath that made her small breasts rise and fall beneath the soft cotton of her blue dress, but her voice sounded strangely thin when she continued, as though the accusation had sucked all the strength out of her. Maybe it was difficult to be forced to admit the truth, even for a woman like her.

'You're talking about Antonio's will, aren't you? And the fact that he left me all that money?'

Becky could feel the tremor that was working its way through her body but she made herself stand rigidly still. Felipe Valdez was watching her and the contempt in his eyes should have hurt or angered her, but in a funny sort of way she suddenly felt detached from what was happening. It was as though she had stepped outside herself and was watching the scene that was being played out in the sunlit grounds of the hospital.

There she stood in her best dress—the one she had chosen especially because she'd hoped it would make the right impression—and there was Felipe standing so tall and straight, his mouth curled into that arrogant smile which a moment ago had seemed to chill her soul.

She found herself wondering what would happen if she blinked—if she would open her eyes and find herself back in the flat in London, waking to the sound of Josh's noisy shouts as he clamoured for her to lift him out of his cot…

She closed her eyes then opened them again, but the scene was just the same. The only difference was that Felipe was now speaking. It was an effort to make sense of what he was saying.

'I see we have made a breakthrough at last. This reluctance to talk about money is so very English. But why pretend that it means nothing when we both know that it is the driving force behind so much that people do?'

He shrugged, his broad shoulders moving lightly beneath the fine wool of his dark grey suit. It was obviously expensive, Becky thought inconsequentially, because it fitted him to perfection, the jacket tailored to accommodate the width of his shoulders and chest, the trimness of his waist.

Her gaze swept lower, taking stock of the long trouser-clad legs, the polished black shoes on his feet. They were handmade, from the look of them, and cut from the softest leather—luxurious, costly. Felipe Valdez obviously saw no reason not to indulge himself and yet he'd seen fit to query what Antonio had done with his inheritance, to question whether his brother had had the right to spend it as he'd wished. Was that what all this antagonism was about—money?

Her eyes rose to his face and she made no attempt to hide her scorn. 'Your brother knew exactly what he wanted to do with his inheritance, Dr Valdez. It was his decision.'

'And you're prepared to swear that you didn't try to influence him in any way? That you didn't take advantage of the fact that he was sick? That you never, *ever,* thought to yourself how wonderful it would be to have all that money at your disposal?'

He laughed when she gasped, deliberately closing his mind to how shocked she looked because he didn't want to have to consider whether or not he was hurting her. 'Or that it would be so much better if Antonio died sooner rather than later so that you wouldn't have to wait quite so long to get your hands on it?'

'No! I can't believe you're saying such things. I *never*

wanted Antonio's money! I *never* tried to influence him to name me in his will. It was his decision, and his alone!'

Becky could feel the bile rushing into her throat and turned away when she realised that she was going to be sick. Stumbling to the flower-bed, she bent over and retched, but she'd had nothing to eat since the previous night so her stomach was mercifully empty.

'Here.'

A tanned hand suddenly appeared, offering her a clean white handkerchief, but she shook her head. She wanted nothing from this man, nothing at all. What a fool she'd been to consider asking him for help. Hadn't Antonio told her that everything had to be on Felipe's terms, that he always had to be in control? Was she really prepared to run the risk of him taking charge of Josh, taking Josh away from her?

The thought steadied her and she stood up straight. Felipe Valdez was watching her and she saw the oddest expression cross his face before the mask of indifference slid back into place.

'Are you feeling better?'

'I'm fine.' She turned and walked towards the path, but he stepped in front of her, putting out a detaining hand when she tried to step around him.

Becky shivered when she felt his cool fingers fastening around her wrist, but she refused to let him think she was afraid by snatching her hand away. She looked up at him with steady eyes and was surprised when she saw a thin line of colour run along his angular cheekbones.

'It would be better if you came into the clinic and rested for a while,' he said shortly.

'I'm fine,' she repeated. She tilted her head so that she could look him straight in the eyes. 'Thank you for the offer, but I have a plane to catch. I shall go straight to the airport. I apologise for disrupting your morning, Dr Valdez.'

She gently withdrew her arm and this time he made no attempt to stop her. Becky walked back along the path and she could feel him watching her every step of the way. She paused when she reached the corner, but the desire to look back was too strong to resist.

He was standing exactly where she'd left him and she felt her heart curl up when she saw the expression on his face. Even from that distance she could see the contempt in his eyes, the disdain.

Her eyes filled with tears but she refused to let him see that he'd upset her. She raised her hand in a mocking salute then carried on, waiting until she was out of sight before finding a tissue and wiping her eyes.

As luck would have it there was a taxi dropping off a fare outside the clinic. Becky flagged it down and asked the driver to take her to the airport. She caught a glimpse of Felipe Valdez as the taxi headed back down the drive, and quickly averted her eyes when he glanced her way.

This would be the first and the last time they ever met because she certainly wouldn't come here again after what had happened today. She was only grateful that she hadn't made the mistake of telling him why she'd come.

Becky sighed as she thought back to that dreadful day when Antonio had told her that his former girlfriend, Tara Lewis, was pregnant with his child and that she intended to get rid of it. It had been a shock for her as well as for him.

Antonio's affair with Tara had been over for some time by then, and he had made no secret of the fact that he regretted having got involved with her. Becky had been a little concerned that he might have been rushing into their own relationship too soon, and had insisted on them taking things slowly at first.

Antonio had had no such reservations, however. He had told Becky that he loved her and that he hoped one day that she might grow to love him in return. Becky had appreciated the fact that he hadn't tried to rush her. She had sensed that she'd been falling in love with him and that all it had needed was a little more time for her own feelings to become clear. Then, just six weeks after they'd started going out together, Antonio had discovered that he had cancer and everything had changed. Time had been the one thing they'd no longer had.

Becky had known from the outset that she wanted to be there for him and had never once wavered in her decision. Antonio had been the sweetest, gentlest man she'd ever known and she'd loved him dearly. When Tara had dropped her bombshell it couldn't have come at a worse time. Antonio had just been told that the treatment he'd needed so desperately would make him sterile, and there Tara had been, telling him that she wanted to abort his child.

He had been close to despair as he'd poured out the whole story to Becky, and that had been when she'd come up with the plan to pay Tara to have the baby. Antonio had inherited a large sum of money on his birthday, so she'd suggested that he use some of that. And then she'd told him that, no matter what happened, she would always take care of the child. It had been that which had convinced him to go ahead.

He and Tara had struck a deal. He would pay her fifty thousand pounds immediately with another fifty thousand when the baby was born, plus an allowance of five thousand pounds each month she was pregnant. If Tara had only stuck to their bargain there wouldn't have been a problem, but there had been constant demands for more money. Becky had hoped that once Tara had received her final payment, that would have been the end of it. But two weeks earlier Tara had turned up at her flat and demanded a further twenty thousand pounds.

Becky simply didn't have that kind of money and had told her so, but Tara had refused to believe her. She'd issued Becky with an ultimatum—either find the money or she would take her to court and claim that she'd been coerced into signing over custody of the baby.

Horrified by the thought of what might happen, Becky had tried to make her see sense. However, Tara had just laughed and told Becky that the courts would probably take Josh into care and then neither one of them would end up with custody of him. As Tara had pointed out, she didn't care what happened to him. She never had. She'd only agreed to give birth to him because Antonio had paid her not to have an abortion.

Becky took a deep breath. She had promised Antonio she

would take care of Josh and she wouldn't let him down. Somehow, some way she would find the money she needed without asking Felipe Valdez for help.

'Everything looks fine, Miss Prentice. There will be some tenderness for a few days, but once the drainage tube has been removed I am confident that you won't have any further problems.'

Felipe stepped back as a nurse drew the sheet over the young woman. Lisa Prentice had been rushed into the Clinica Valdez with a seriously inflamed appendix. Felipe's colleague, Silvia Ramirez, had performed the operation, and now he turned to her.

'An excellent job, Dr Ramirez, performed under very difficult circumstances. I believe the appendix was ready to burst.'

'That's correct, sir,' Silvia replied, smiling with pleasure at the compliment. She was an attractive brunette in her thirties, engaged to be married to another doctor on the surgical team which Felipe headed. He appreciated the fact that neither of them had allowed their relationship to intrude into their work, although he would have had no hesitation in doing something about it if it had. The welfare of the patients they treated at the Clinica Valdez came first and foremost, and always would.

'Another half-hour and the outcome might not have been quite so fortunate. *Sí?*' He turned to the young woman in the bed once again and frowned.

'Did you have no indication that there might be something wrong before you set out on your holiday, Miss Prentice? I find it strange that you experienced no discomfort.'

Lisa flushed when she heard the scepticism in his voice. She was a pretty girl in her teens and had come on holiday to Mallorca with a group of her friends. Felipe couldn't fail to see how uncomfortable she looked about having to answer the question.

'I did have a few twinges the night before we were due to fly over here,' she muttered. 'I just hoped it was indigestion or something.'

'I see.' His black brows swooped upwards as he regarded her with cool, brown eyes. 'It never occurred to you that it might be something more serious and that perhaps you should visit your doctor before you set off on your holiday?'

'Not really. I mean, if Mum had found out that I wasn't feeling too good she might have stopped me going...' She tailed off uncertainly.

Felipe bit back a sigh. The young woman had preferred to run the risk of being seriously ill rather than cancel her holiday. It would take more than the promise of two weeks in the sun to get him on a plane if he were feeling under the weather.

That thought reminded him of what had happened earlier in the day, and he frowned. Had Rebecca Williams been feeling ill before she'd come to see him or had it been what he'd said that had had such disastrous consequences? Even the most consummate actress couldn't have faked that bout of sickness, and it troubled him to know that he might have been responsible for it, troubled him more than it should, too. Why should he care about the wretched woman after the way she had used his brother?

His brows drew even further together and he saw Silvia glance rather nervously at him. She was obviously wondering if she'd done something to cause his displeasure so he quickly smoothed his features into their customary bland mask.

'May I suggest that the next time you go on holiday you are a little more sensible, Miss Prentice? As it is you will not get to enjoy very much of your stay on the island, I'm afraid. We shall keep you here for the next two to three days then I shall recommend to your insurance company that you should be flown home immediately.'

'Oh! I didn't realise I would have to go home.' Tears filled the girl's eyes. 'I thought I would be able to join my friends. We've been saving up for this holiday for months, you see, and now I won't have a chance to enjoy any of it.'

Felipe sighed, although he couldn't help wondering why the sight of the girl's tears should have moved him. He wasn't uncaring about the people he treated, but he'd learned a long time ago to distance himself. It puzzled him that he didn't seem able to do so right then...

Unless it was that meeting with Rebecca Williams which had allowed his emotions to surface?

It was a deeply disquieting thought and he ruthlessly drove it out of his mind. 'I feel that it would be far more sensible if you returned home as soon as you are discharged from the clinic, Miss Prentice. However...' He held up his hand when Lisa started to say something and was unsurprised when she fell silent. Few people stood up to him, he'd found, although whether that was a good thing was open to question. Maybe he would be a better person if occasionally he had to bow to another person's will? He couldn't remember the last time anyone had contradicted him—apart from Rebecca Williams, of course.

It was an effort to hide his dismay as that thought slid into his mind, but hiding his feelings was something he was particularly good at. '*However*, I am prepared to review your case in a few days' time.'

He shrugged when he heard the young woman's gasp of delight, clamping down on the urge to smile at her because it wouldn't be right to let her think that his agreement was a foregone conclusion. 'If you continue making such excellent progress it might be possible to allow you to carry on with your holiday—with certain provisos, of course.'

'Oh, thank you, Dr Valdez, and you, too, Dr Ramirez. That's just brilliant news!'

Lisa was beaming when they moved away from her bed. Felipe sensed that Silvia was looking at him and glanced at her. 'You disagree with my decision, Dr Ramirez? Please, feel free to say so if you do.'

'Not at all,' she said quickly. He saw a little colour touch her cheeks and sighed when it struck him what was wrong. Silvia was surprised because he'd changed his mind. Frankly, it was unheard of for him to go back on a decision once he had made it.

It made him wonder what was wrong with him that day and

why he seemed to be acting so out of character. He had changed his mind about sending Lisa home once she was discharged and now he found himself wishing that he'd discovered what Rebecca Williams had wanted. It had seemed enough at the time that he'd been able to tell her what he thought of her, but all of a sudden he was beset by curiosity.

Why *had* she come to see him? He'd heard her telling the taxi-driver to take her to the airport so had it been a sudden whim that had made her spend her last few hours on the island visiting him, or had there been another reason behind it?

The question nagged at him for the rest of the day so that by the time he left the hospital he was tired of thinking about it. He made his way from the main building and followed the path through the trees until he came to a pink-washed villa. It was almost seven and the sun was sinking low in the sky, casting a burnished haze across the bay.

Felipe paused as he always did to admire the view, but that evening it didn't soothe him. He felt too on edge and keyed up, a feeling of tension making his nerves hum. It had been years since he'd felt that way. The last time had been when he'd found out that his fiancée had been cheating on him.

He'd solved that problem by ending the engagement and hadn't made the mistake of getting involved with anyone ever since. Any relationships he'd had in the intervening years had meant little to him apart from physically. If only he could apply the same objectivity to what had happened that day, but wondering what Rebecca Williams had wanted was eating away at him.

He let himself into the villa, bypassing the dining-room where his housekeeper had left his supper in the heated serving trolley. Usually he enjoyed her cooking but that night the smell of meat and vegetables made him feel sick, although not as sick as Rebecca had been that morning.

'Madre de Dios!' He slammed his hand against the study door, feeling pain shoot through his palm when it connected with the ornately carved wood. It stunned him to feel it and

know that he was capable of such anger when he had always—
always—been able to control his emotions before.

But this was different. This all had to do with Antonio, and
there were too many emotions churning inside him. He felt
guilt and anger, grief and pain, all laced with a deep contempt
for the way that woman had used his brother when he had been
so vulnerable.

Antonio hadn't deserved to be treated like that!

Tears stung Felipe's eyes but he blinked them away. In his
heart he knew that he might be making a mistake, but he didn't
have a choice. He had to sort this out once and for all, bring
everything to its rightful conclusion. Rebecca Williams must
be made to pay.

He went to his desk and picked up the phone, his hand was
rock steady when he dialled the number. It was the usual push-
button service but he obeyed each command without experi-
encing his usual irritation until, finally, he was connected to an
operator.

'I wish to book a seat on the next flight to London. My
name? Valdez, Dr Felipe Valdez.'

CHAPTER TWO

'YOU'VE not got much of a suntan, I must say. Don't tell me it was raining in Mallorca?'

Becky glanced round as her friend, Karen Hardy, came into the staffroom where she'd been making a cup of coffee. It had been a hectic morning on the paediatric intensive care unit of St Leonard's Hospital, where she worked, and it was the first opportunity she'd had to take a break. She automatically reached for the jar of coffee and made Karen a drink as well.

'It wasn't raining, but I didn't get much chance to enjoy the sun,' she explained, handing her friend the mug.

She picked up her own cup, hoping that the hot coffee would help to warm away the chill which seemed to have invaded her since the previous day. She'd felt cold ever since she had got back from Mallorca despite the fact that the weather in London was surprisingly warm for the time of year. But maybe the chill she felt owed itself less to the outside temperature than to the frosty reception she had received at the Clinica Valdez.

Her grey eyes clouded as she recalled what Felipe Valdez had said to her. She had spent the night going over and over every cruel word, but nothing seemed to take the sting out of them. He honestly believed that she had *used* Antonio for her own ends. The thought still made her feel ill.

'Hey, are you OK? You look as though you'd just swallowed something nasty.' Karen sniffed her coffee suspiciously. 'The milk isn't off again, is it?'

'No, it's fine. Don't worry, I'm not trying to poison you,' Becky quickly assured her. 'Here have one of these.'

She offered Karen the packet of chocolate biscuits which one of the doctors on the unit had given her in the hope that it would distract her from asking anything else. Karen was a good

friend but Becky had deemed it wiser not to tell anyone too
much since she'd taken the job at St Leonard's. People would
have been bound to gossip if the truth had got out, and that
was the last thing she wanted to happen.

She'd told everyone the story that she and Antonio had decided upon—that she was a single mother, bringing up her
nine-month-old son on her own. Whenever anyone asked about
Josh's father, she answered quite truthfully that he had died
not long after the baby had been born.

Everyone had accepted it without question, and although she
occasionally felt guilty about having to deceive them she felt
she didn't have a choice. She wouldn't take any risks where
Josh was concerned.

'Thanks.' Karen took a biscuit and carried on talking through
a mouthful of crumbs. 'So why didn't you get much chance to
enjoy the sun while you were in Mallorca?'

'Oh, it was just a flying visit. I was there and back within a
day.'

'Really?' Karen made no attempt to hide her surprise. Her
blue eyes gleamed with curiosity as she stared at Becky. 'You
must have had a very good reason for not stopping. I mean,
it's a long way to go just for a few hours, isn't it?'

Becky sighed as she realised her mistake. She shouldn't have
said that because her friend wouldn't have been any the wiser
if she'd let her believe that she had stayed in Mallorca. She'd
had five days' leave owing to her and had planned the trip to
coincide with them. Not for the first time she rued the fact that
being deceitful didn't come naturally to her. Even when speaking to Felipe Valdez she had needed to watch every word she'd
said.

'I had something to sort out,' she replied quickly, not wanting to dwell on the previous day's events. Recalling the contempt on Felipe's face still had the power to upset her, even
though she didn't understand why his opinion should carry any
weight. So long as Josh was safe, nothing else mattered. And
once she found the money she needed to pay Tara, her biggest
problem would have been solved.

'Something to do with Josh, do you mean?' Karen guessed astutely. 'You mentioned something about his father coming from Mallorca—did you go there to see his family?'

'That's right.' Becky shrugged. 'As I said, it was just a flying visit—that's why I didn't stay very long. Anyway, I wanted to get home to Josh.'

'You didn't take him with you?'

She groaned when she heard the surprise in Karen's voice. What was that saying about the tangled webs we weave? One lie seemed to lead to another and if she wasn't careful she would start tripping herself up.

'He had an ear infection so I didn't think it would be wise to take him on the plane. He stayed with the childminder so he was perfectly happy.'

She could tell that Karen was going to ask her something else so it was a relief when their new trainee nurse, Debbie Rothwell, put her head round the door.

'I'm awfully sorry, Becky, but can you come? Holly is crying and I've no idea what's wrong with her. All the monitor readings are fine. I've double-checked.'

Becky put her cup on the draining-board and smiled at the younger woman. Debbie was still very nervous about the responsibility involved with working in the IC unit and rarely trusted her instincts where the children were concerned. Whilst the monitoring equipment was invaluable it didn't supply all the answers.

'Have you tried asking her what's wrong?'

'Well, no, I haven't, actually,' Debbie admitted, looking even more flustered. 'I suppose I should have thought of that first.'

'Don't worry. It takes a while to slot into the routine here,' Becky said kindly, going to the door. 'Let's go and have a look at Holly and see if we can find out what's the matter with her. She's due to be transferred to a ward once Mr Watts has seen her, so there's no need to be overly concerned. She's well on the mend, I'm glad to say.'

They made their way into the IC unit and went straight to

Holly Benson's bed. The four year-old had been admitted the previous week after suffering a stroke. She had been gravely ill at the time and the prognosis hadn't been good. However, dedicated nursing care, plus the child's own will to survive, had pulled her through.

The good news was that young children were known to make an excellent recovery after they'd suffered a stroke. Nobody was exactly sure how it worked, but it had been proved that other parts of the brain took over the tasks performed by any damaged areas. With a bit of luck, little Holly would lead a full and active life.

'Now then, sweetheart, what's the matter? Does your head hurt or do you have a pain anywhere?' she asked gently, bending down beside the child's bed.

Although Holly had been removed from most of the monitoring equipment, she was still attached to the machine that was checking her blood pressure and heart rate. Becky saw the child pluck at the leads attached to her, and gently moved Holly's hand away so that she couldn't dislodge them.

'Want to get up,' the little girl said, her lower lip pouting. 'Want to play!'

'Oh, I see!'

She laughed as she kissed the little girl's cheek, thinking what a good sign that was. When a child was fretting because she wanted to get out of bed, she had to be on the mend.

'I'm afraid you can't get up just yet, poppet. The doctor has to see how you are first.'

She turned to Debbie and grinned when she saw the relief on the young nurse's face. 'Panic over. How do you fancy reading Holly a story while we wait for Mr Watts to make his appearance? I wouldn't like him to think that we don't keep our patients happy while they're with us.'

She moved away from the bed after both Holly and Debbie had agreed that it sounded like the perfect solution and made her way down the ward, automatically checking each child as she passed. There were ten beds in the paediatric intensive care unit and every one of them was in use. She had no doubt that the minute Holly was transferred to the medical ward, another young patient would arrive.

St Leonard's was the only paediatric intensive care unit in that area of London, and beds there were always at a premium. It meant that her role as a staff nurse was a demanding one, but she'd never regretted her decision to work there. The fact that she'd been able to choose to work permanent days had been a real bonus because she didn't know how she would have managed to look after Josh if she'd had to work shifts.

A smile softened her mouth as she thought about the little boy. Even though it was a huge responsibility, she had never regretted offering to take care of him. Josh was Antonio's son and doubly precious because of that. She couldn't have loved any child more than she loved him.

Becky left the ward and went to the office. Sister Reece was on holiday that week so Becky was in charge in her absence and there was a stack of paperwork to catch up with. She opened the office door then froze when she caught sight of the man standing by the window. For one horrible moment she thought she was going to faint as the floor seemed to rush up to meet her.

She saw him turn, saw the concern that crossed his face, saw him take a step towards her—and it was that which steadied her. The thought of Felipe Valdez actually touching her was more than she could bear.

'Don't!'

Felipe froze when he heard the total rejection in Rebecca's voice. Frankly, he wasn't sure what to do. She looked as though she was ready to keel over, yet the expression on her face dared him to go to her assistance.

He took a deep breath while he tried to think, but it was surprisingly difficult to assess the situation. Knowing that he was the object of all those waves of antipathy that were flowing across the room had thrown him off course. He could no longer take a rational view of what was happening and it shocked him to realise that he was in danger of acting instinctively and without thought.

'What do you want?'

Her voice sounded cold and sharp, as though all the warmth and sweetness had been drained from it, and he frowned because it was strangely distressing to know that he was responsible for the change. He found himself wondering if he should apologise for what he had done before common sense reasserted itself. If there was any apologising to be done, it needed to come from her, not him.

'I want to know why you came to see me yesterday.'

He saw her slender body stiffen but he refused to let himself be swayed by this act she was putting on. He had known that she was a nurse because Antonio had told him that in his last letter, but it had been a shock to discover that she worked in one of the most demanding departments in any hospital.

When he'd called at the house where she lived, a neighbour had told him that Rebecca worked in the paediatric intensive care unit of St Leonard's Hospital. He had taken a taxi there, trying to reconcile himself to the thought of her doing such a demanding job. Yet why should he have been so surprised? Who better than Rebecca Williams to deal with sick children when she was incapable of feeling any genuine emotion? The thought made his heart ache for some reason.

'You must have had a very good reason for coming to see me, Miss Williams, and I want to know what it was. Although maybe I could make an educated guess.'

'I don't know what you mean,' she said quickly, but he could see the fear that had darkened her eyes. 'I told you that I just wanted to meet you—'

'And it was a lie.'

He smiled sardonically when she fell silent, wondering why he couldn't seem to derive any pleasure from her discomfort. It felt on a par with pulling the wings off a butterfly to stand there and mock her, but he couldn't afford to weaken, wouldn't allow himself to forget what had driven him to come. He just had to think about Antonio and anything…*anything*…was justified!

'Please, don't insult my intelligence, Miss Williams. We

both know that you wanted something from me. Was it money that you were after, by any chance?'

He glanced around the room, fighting the feeling of sickness that was welling inside him because he knew his suspicions had been correct. She *had* come to see him to ask for money and the proof of that was the way she stood there without making any attempt to deny the accusation.

It was an effort to look at her again because he didn't think he had ever felt more angry than he did at that moment. 'Have you spent what Antonio left you already? Is that why you're working here when you should be living in the lap of luxury?'

He shook his head reprovingly, determined not to let her know how much it disturbed him to see her looking so shocked. Why should he care about her feelings when she'd cared so little about Antonio's? It didn't make sense.

'I'm not sure exactly how much my brother left you. Our parents put two hundred thousand pounds in a trust fund for Antonio, for when he reached the age of twenty-five. I doubt he had the time to spend very much of it before he died, so you must have received quite a considerable sum. Yet you have managed to spend it all in a few short months, apparently.'

He smiled thinly, wondering why she didn't try to justify her actions, although maybe she knew how pointless it would be to try and play on his sympathy. It might have worked in the past because he could understand that many men must have been taken in by her beauty. Even he was aware of it and could feel himself responding on a purely physical level.

No man could look at Rebecca Williams and not want her. Even though he despised everything she stood for, he could feel a stirring in his blood. Her delicate beauty and that air of vulnerability she projected was a potent mixture and he could understand how his brother had been fooled by it. However, that was where he and Antonio differed. *He* knew that beneath the beautiful outer shell was a woman who would stop at nothing to get what she wanted. And what she wanted most of all was money.

'I almost feel sorry for you, because I'm sure that working

for your living wasn't part of your plan.' His voice grated because the thought seemed to sear right through him. All she'd ever wanted from Antonio had been his money!

'Nevertheless, I'm very much afraid that I shall have to disappoint you even further because you won't get a penny out of me. I am not my brother. I am not as gullible as poor Antonio was!'

He brushed past her, feeling the tremor that coursed through his body when his arm brushed her shoulder. Revulsion, he told himself as he went to the door, simple revulsion—if anything to do with this woman could be classed as simple. He had no idea how she'd hoped to extract money from him, but he couldn't bear to question her further. Finding out more about Rebecca Williams's sordid life certainly wouldn't make him feel any better.

'Becky, can you come—? Oops, sorry. I didn't know you were busy.'

Felipe ground to a halt when a nurse suddenly appeared. He saw her look curiously at him before she turned to Rebecca and spoke more formally this time.

'Mr Watts is on his way. I thought I'd better warn you because he's in a rush. Something about having to go to Leeds to give a lecture this evening, or so Simon said.'

'Thank you, Karen. I'll be right there.'

Felipe flinched when she spoke, wondering what had caused that ripple to run through him. He shot her an uneasy glance over his shoulder but she wasn't looking at him. She took a stack of folders off the desk and went to the door, all the time avoiding eye contact with him.

She smiled as she handed the notes to the nurse, but Felipe could tell the effort it cost her to act as though nothing was wrong. All of a sudden, he wished that he hadn't come because he'd achieved nothing from his visit. He'd simply upset himself and upset Rebecca, too.

Oddly, that last thought was the most disturbing of all. Hurting Rebecca hadn't given him any satisfaction, as he'd hoped it would. It was an effort to hide his dismay when Rebecca addressed the other woman in a cool little voice that told him just how difficult she had found the past few minutes.

'Check that all the obs are up to date, will you, Karen? You know how Mr Watts hates it if everything isn't spot on.'

'Do I ever!' The nurse took the bundle then looked worriedly at Rebecca. 'You will be there when he arrives? I don't think I'm up to coping with one of his high-speed ward rounds.'

'Of course. Dr Valdez was just leaving so I won't be long.'

'*Valdez!* Oh, I didn't realise.' The young nurse laughed as she turned to him. 'What an idiot I am! I should have known the minute I saw you.'

She gave him a considering look. 'Yes, I can see the resemblance now, especially around the eyes. Josh has exactly the same colour eyes as you have. Isn't it amazing how something like eye colour can be passed on through a family?'

Felipe didn't know what to say. He knew that she was waiting for him to answer, but there was no way that he could have formed even the simplest sentence.

He turned to Rebecca and this time she was looking straight at him—staring at him, to be precise. Her eyes seemed to be riveted to his face and the expression in them made his heart race. He had never seen such fear in anyone's eyes before.

He heard the door close as the nurse hurriedly left, and almost laughed out loud. It was obvious that she was trying to be tactful because she'd sensed that she might have said something wrong, but it was far too late for that now. With a few unguarded words his life had been turned on its head.

'Who is Josh?'

He didn't realise the question had come from his lips at first because it hadn't sounded like his voice. It had sounded too strained, too raw, too full of emotion to be the voice of Felipe Valdez. He saw Rebecca swallow, watched her mouth open and struggled to concentrate because it was vitally important that he heard what she said.

'Josh is my son.'

She paused and he knew that he was holding his breath as he waited for her to continue. 'He's Antonio's son, too.'

Becky could feel her heart beating, but it felt as though time had suddenly come to a halt. Felipe was standing stock still and the expression of shock on his face would have made her laugh if there had been anything remotely funny about the situation.

She saw him swallow and tried to prepare herself for what he would ask her. He would be bound to have questions—dozens of them—and she needed to decide what to tell him. But it was hard to think when her brain felt as though it had seized up.

'My...my brother had a child...a son?'

Her heart ached with a sudden, fierce pain when she heard the bewilderment in his voice. For some reason she wanted to make this as easy as possible for him, even though she knew how dangerous it was to consider his feelings. One small slip, one unguarded word and the situation could spiral out of control.

'Yes. His name is Josh and he's nine months old,' she told him quietly. 'He looks very like Antonio and you, too, I suppose.'

She gave him a tentative smile, watching the rapid play of emotions that crossed his face as he struggled to make sense of what she was saying. 'He definitely has your colour eyes, as Karen just mentioned. Antonio's eyes were a lot darker.'

'Antonio took after our mother,' he said roughly. 'I favour my father's side of the family.'

'But there's still a strong resemblance between you both.' She felt her heart catch because until then she really hadn't been aware of the similarities between the two brothers. Now it scared her to realise how alike they were. The last thing she could afford was to look at Felipe and see Antonio. She had to remember that they were two very different people.

It was a relief when there was a knock on the door because she desperately needed some time to think about what had happened. She hurried to answer it, shaking her head when Debbie apologised for the interruption.

'It's fine, really. Don't worry. Has Mr Watts arrived?'

'Yes. Karen sent me to tell you.' Debbie shot a curious glance at Felipe then lowered her voice. 'He's none too pleased because you weren't there to meet him, I'm afraid, Becky.'

'I'll be straight there,' she assured her.

She closed the door then felt her heart skip a beat when she turned and found Felipe standing right behind her. He was so close that she could smell the tangy scent of his aftershave, feel the heat of his body, and all of a sudden it felt as though her senses were being swamped by him.

'I have to go,' she explained, quickly moving away. She went to the desk and picked up a pen, trying her best not to let him see how nervous she was all of a sudden. She had never felt like this around Antonio, never once felt so deeply aware of him as she was of his brother. The idea worried her for a moment until it struck her that it was because Antonio had never presented a threat to her, like Felipe did.

'I have to get back to work,' she said more calmly, relieved to have found such a simple explanation.

'But we need to talk, Rebecca. That is obvious. *Sí?*'

He had phrased it as a question, but Becky knew there wasn't the slightest chance that he would let her refuse. He wanted to know all about Josh, and who could blame him?

Finding out that he was an uncle had come as a shock to him, but it was what happened from here on that frightened her most. She was under no illusions as to how Felipe felt about her. He might be struggling to come to terms with what had happened at the moment, but it wouldn't be long before the implications of it hit him.

How would he feel about her being Josh's mother? Maybe he would have to accept it while he believed that Josh really was her child, but if the truth ever emerged it would be a very different story. There wasn't a doubt in her mind that Felipe would waste no time trying to remove her from his nephew's life.

She bit her lip as the irony of the situation struck her. A few days ago she had seen Felipe Valdez as her only hope to stop

Josh being taken away from her. Now he presented as big a threat as Tara did.

It was an effort to contain her panic, but she couldn't afford to give in to it. She carefully wiped all expression from her face when Felipe spoke.

'This is the address and telephone number of the hotel where I am staying. I shall expect you to call me as soon as you are free.' He took a notebook from his jacket pocket and wrote down the details then tore off the sheet and handed it to her. 'We need to arrange a time this evening when we can meet.'

'But I don't finish work until six,' she protested, knowing that she needed more time to work out what she should tell him.

'Six o'clock will be fine. I shall expect you to call me then. To be perfectly blunt, Miss Williams, I am not prepared to wait while you choose a time that is more convenient for you.'

He didn't say anything else before he left. Becky heard his footsteps echoing along the corridor and shuddered as reaction set in. She took a deep breath, but the feeling of panic was getting worse.

Maybe it was understandable that he should want to know all about his brother's child, but she didn't dare think about how difficult it was going to be, explaining everything to him. How much could she really afford to tell him?

It was an effort to put that thought out of her mind as she hurried into the ward. James Watts, the consultant in charge of the IC unit, was waiting by the door with his party, and he greeted her with noticeable coolness.

'Ah, there you are, Staff. Good of you to join us. If we're all here at last, shall we get started? I have to be in Sheffield by five, and the last thing I need are any more delays.'

Becky hastily apologised, feeling suitably rebuked. They went straight to Danny Epstein's bed and she handed James the boy's notes. Danny had been admitted a few days earlier with severe endocarditis—inflammation of the internal lining of the heart—and he was still giving them cause for concern. She waited by the bed while James read through the night staff's report in his usual thorough fashion. Although the consultant had brought several students with him that morning, as well as his two registrars, it was very quiet. Nobody dared to interrupt him or they would suffer the consequences.

Becky found her thoughts drifting back to what had happened in the office as the silence lengthened. What would be the best way to handle this coming meeting with Felipe? He was bound to have a lot of questions and she had to find a way to answer them without arousing his suspicions—

'We'll continue the high-dose antibiotics and hope that they'll clear things up eventually… Staff?'

She blinked as James Watts paused and peered at her over the top of his spectacles. A wash of colour ran up her face when she saw Simon Montague, the senior registrar, treat her to a conspiratorial grin. It must have been obvious to everyone that she hadn't been paying attention, and it alarmed her that she had allowed her own problems to intrude on her work.

'I'll mark that down on Danny's card,' she said, hurriedly thinking back over what the consultant had said. 'Is the cardio team planning on replacing the damaged heart valves soon?'

'Once we have the infection under control,' James replied shortly, making sure she knew that he didn't appreciate it when members of his staff failed to give him their undivided attention.

Becky breathed a sigh of relief when James turned to the students and began to outline the boy's case history. She'd got off pretty lightly, bearing in mind that she'd already provoked the consultant's wrath once that day.

'This young fellow caught an infection whilst having a tooth extracted,' James explained. He paused, the students hanging on his every word. 'Lo and behold, a few days later he came down with endocarditis. We know for certain that two of the valves have been damaged, but we shall have to wait and see how badly the rest have been affected.'

Becky gathered together the notes as the students exclaimed in amazement. They were in their first year at medical school and it was obvious they'd never realised that having a tooth out could be such a risky procedure. James had played up the dangers for dramatic effect, but at least it had helped to restore his good humour when his audience had responded as he'd hoped.

'OK, so what's wrong? You look as though you've got the weight of the world on your shoulders.' Simon hung back to talk to her as the others moved to the next bed.

Becky sighed inwardly when she saw the concern on his face. Simon was really nice and if it had been anything else worrying her she might have been tempted to unburden herself. However, there was no way that she could tell him what was wrong that day.

'Nothing's wrong. I'm fine,' she began, then looked round when James coughed. She flushed again when he treated her to another frosty stare.

'I *would* like to finish this round some time today, Staff. So if you and Dr Montague would be kind enough to join us, I shall be eternally grateful.'

'I'm sorry, sir,' she said, hurrying over to join him. She could tell that Simon hadn't believed her, but she decided that it would be simpler to let the subject drop. Although she wouldn't like to offend Simon, he really wasn't her priority at the moment.

She purposely drove all thoughts of Felipe Valdez out of her head while they completed the round then hurried to the office and busied herself with phoning through an order to the supplies department so that she could avoid having to speak to Simon again. He poked his head round the door and mouthed that he would catch her later then hurried away.

Becky sighed as she hung up. What *was* she going to do? Felipe now knew about Josh even though he wasn't in possession of all the facts. But exactly how much should she tell him?

It was impossible to answer that question because so much depended on what Felipe intended to do. However, it did make her see how foolish it would be not to phone him as soon as she got home from work. Felipe Valdez wasn't the kind of man who would simply disappear from her life because she wanted him to.

She frowned. Was that really what she wanted, though? Did she honestly wish that she would never have to see him again?

The answer should have been a resounding *yes*. Felipe was undoubtedly a threat to her and Josh, but her feelings towards him weren't as clear-cut as they should have been.

Felipe couldn't relax. For the past three hours he'd done nothing but pace his hotel room. Everything he'd learned kept whirling around inside his head and he couldn't make sense of it.

Antonio had had a child with Rebecca Williams. A son. Was it true? Or was it another one of her schemes, another lie to add to the web of deceit that surrounded her?

He sank onto a chair and picked up the phone then sat and stared at it. He knew the number of the hospital by heart, but should he phone her or wait until she phoned him? He had to decide what he intended to ask her first. If she still maintained that the child—Josh, she'd called him—was Antonio's son, surely he needed proof. Who knew how many men Rebecca Williams might have slept with? Any one of them could be the child's father...

Only he had a gut feeling that wasn't the case. Rebecca's son was also his brother's child, the only thing left on this earth that could provide a tangible link to Antonio. By heaven, he wasn't going to sit there and phone her or wait for her to contact him. He was going to see her again, and this time he intended to find out exactly what was going on.

A thin smile curved his mouth. He only hoped that Rebecca wouldn't try to lie to him because it would be a mistake.

Becky was late leaving the hospital because there had been a crisis when Danny Epstein had arrested. It had taken the combined efforts of the whole team to stabilise him and he had now been sent to Theatre to have two badly damaged heart valves replaced.

Whether he would survive the operation in his weakened state was in the lap of the gods, but it was his only chance and she applauded his parents' decision to take it. It wasn't easy being a parent, as she had discovered.

A smile tilted her lips as she hurried out of the main doors. She loved collecting Josh at the end of the day because he was always so happy to see her. The little boy had a wonderfully sunny nature, which had made him rather a pet of the childminder who looked after him while she was at work. It was reassuring to know that he was being well cared for when she couldn't be with him.

'Miss Williams.'

She stopped dead when she recognised the voice that had called her name. She'd known that Felipe wouldn't rest until he'd got to the bottom of this situation, but she'd hoped to have a little more time before she spoke to him again. Now, when she turned and saw the uncompromising expression on his face, she felt her heart start to race.

Would she be able to stop him finding out that she wasn't Josh's real mother? Everything hinged on her doing that.

CHAPTER THREE

'I NEED to speak to you, Miss Williams. There's a bar across the road—maybe we can go there.'

'I can't.'

Felipe frowned when he heard the anxiety in Rebecca's voice. Although he understood how stressful this situation must be for her he couldn't understand why she sounded so scared.

Once again the idea that she might have been telling him a pack of lies about the child being Antonio's son filled his mind. After all, why hadn't Antonio written and told him that he'd become a father? Despite that row they'd had before Antonio had left Mallorca, his brother had never been the kind of person to harbour a grudge. There was something about this situation which didn't add up.

'Can't or won't?' he said tersely. 'I'm having a great deal of difficulty understanding what is going on, Miss Williams. A few hours ago you told me that you and my brother had had a son and now you refuse to talk to me about the child.'

Her lids lowered, effectively hiding her eyes from view. 'I'm not refusing to talk to you, Dr Valdez.' She shrugged, but he wasn't blind to the strain that was etched on her face when she glanced up. 'However, I thought we'd agreed that I would telephone you and arrange a time when we could meet.'

'We did, but I can see no reason why we cannot talk now and get this all sorted out.' He went to slide his hand under her elbow, but she stepped smartly out of reach.

'I've just told you that I can't talk to you now. I have to collect Josh. I'm late as it is because we had an emergency, and the childminder will be wondering where I am.'

She started hurrying down the path, but if she thought that he was prepared to let her walk away, she was mistaken. Who knew what she might be planning? She claimed that she'd intended to phone him, but could he trust her? What if she took Josh and disappeared? How would he feel if his brother's only child was left in the care of a woman like her?

He strode after her, his long legs swiftly bringing him level with her. He saw her glance round, saw her pretty mouth compress, but she didn't say a word. They walked in silence down the path and across the busy London street. It was the middle of the rush hour and the traffic was horrendous, car after car belching out fumes.

He suddenly wished that he was back home in Mallorca, breathing in the fresh, salt-laden air as it blew in from the bay. Had Antonio really preferred to exchange all that beauty for this?

'Antonio used to love the rush hour. He spent a lot of time looking out of the window when...when he became too weak to go out.'

He heard the catch in her voice and felt his heart ache. He had tried many times to imagine how his brother must have felt, knowing that he was dying. Suddenly, he needed to know how Antonio had dealt with it.

'How was he toward the end?' He heard the roughness in his voice and knew that she had heard it, too, but, oddly, he didn't feel embarrassed. He cleared his throat, deeply disturbed by the thought. 'It must have been difficult for him to come to terms with the fact that he was dying.'

'I think by that time he had come to accept what was going to happen.' She smiled gently. 'He told me that he didn't want to waste his last few weeks on earth by feeling bitter. And, of course, having Josh helped tremendously. Knowing that a little bit of him would live on after his death gave him strength.'

'Did he see the child, then?' Felipe asked, keeping his gaze averted because he was deeply moved by what she had said. He wasn't embarrassed, but he was too private a person to feel completely comfortable about exposing his feelings.

The problem was that it was so hard to think about Antonio at the end of his life; he kept having flashbacks to when he'd been born. Felipe had been fifteen when his brother had arrived in the world. His parents had been shocked at first when they'd discovered they were having another child and delighted later when the baby had been born.

Antonio had brought great joy to his parent's lives, great joy to his own life as well. After their parents had been killed in a car accident when Antonio was ten, Felipe had willingly taken over the task of raising him.

He had done his best to guide Antonio, but maybe he'd been too strict. If he hadn't been so set on making Antonio do as he'd wanted him to, his brother might never have left Mallorca and certainly wouldn't have ended up having a child with Rebecca Williams. How strange it was the way everything had worked out.

'Oh, yes. Josh was born a few weeks before...well, before Antonio died. He was in a lot of pain by then and his medication had been increased because of it. He used to sleep most of the time, but once I brought Josh home from hospital Antonio refused to take more than the barest minimum of pain relief.'

He saw her dash her hand across her eyes and could hear how her voice had thickened with tears. 'He said that he didn't want to miss a single minute he had left with Josh. He used to hold him all day long. My one abiding memory of Antonio is seeing him sitting by the window, cradling his son in his arms.'

Her voice broke on a sob and it seemed the most natural thing in the world to take her in his arms and hold her while she cried. In his heart, Felipe knew that he was probably making a mistake, but he couldn't stop himself wanting to comfort her.

He drew her closer, amazed by the sense of helplessness he felt. He couldn't assuage her grief and for some reason it hurt to know that she was crying for his brother and that there wasn't a thing he could do about it.

He smoothed his hand over her hair, feeling the silky strands snagging against his palm. Her hair felt like gossamer, so light, so soft, so sensuous. He found himself staring at it in wonderment, watching the play of light and shadow as the pale gold strands rippled beneath his fingers. All of a sudden he wished that this moment could last for ever, that he could keep her here in his arms and never let her go. She would be safe then, because he would be able to protect her from any more pain.

A shiver ran through him and he stiffened, shocked that he should be thinking thoughts like that. This was Rebecca Williams in his arms, not some woman with whom he was thinking of having an affair. It was a relief when she abruptly stepped back so that he was forced to release her.

'I'm sorry. I didn't mean to do that,' she said softly, her voice quavering, although whether it was from embarrassment or pleasure at him having held her he couldn't decide.

He took a deep breath and deliberately rid himself of that foolish notion before it had a chance to take hold. Rebecca was wiping her eyes with a tissue and there was a strangely touching dignity about the way she stood up straighter once she had finished.

All of a sudden it struck him that she possessed certain qualities he had never expected, and it worried him to realise that he might have misjudged her when he'd been so sure that he knew everything that he needed to know. Was Rebecca really the scheming, self-serving woman he'd believed her to be? Or had he been wrong about her?

Suddenly, it seemed equally important that he find out the answer to those questions, too.

Becky took a deep breath, but she felt such a fool for breaking down. She shot a wary glance at Felipe but, surprisingly, there was no sign of the contempt which she had expected to see on his face.

Her heart gave a painful lurch as she recalled how good it had felt when he'd held her in his arms. His body had felt so strong as he'd cradled her against him. She'd had an overwhelming urge to lean on him and keep on leaning. The past year had been so hard and it would be wonderful to be able to share this burden...

But dangerous.

What would Felipe do if he found out the truth about Josh? Antonio had signed a document appointing her as the child's legal guardian, and had got Tara to sign it, too, but would it hold up in a court of law?

That had been her fear all along, that her claim on Josh might be overruled. Antonio's solicitor had warned them that there was always a chance of that happening, that nothing—not even a legal document—was guaranteed in this kind of a situation.

That was why she'd panicked when Tara had threatened her, yet the thought that, unwittingly, she might have put herself and Josh in even more danger filled her with dread. No matter how wonderful it had felt to have him comfort her, she had to remember that Felipe was her enemy.

'I don't usually go to pieces like that,' she said stiffly. She didn't want to think of him as her enemy, although she wasn't sure why. She felt a ripple of alarm scurry through her when she saw his eyes suddenly narrow.

'I don't imagine that you usually find yourself in a position like this, Miss Williams, so, please, don't apologise. Unfortunately, we cannot always predict how we will react.'

She wasn't sure what he had meant by that, and frowned. Was Felipe admitting that he had reacted strangely by taking her in his arms and trying to comfort her perhaps?

Now she thought about it, it was a strange thing for him to have done. Maybe she had difficulty thinking of him as her enemy, but surely he didn't have any problems with the idea? And yet he had held her with such tenderness, such gentleness that it hadn't felt as though he hated her.

The thought bothered her probably more than it should have done. She tried to put it out of her head as she started walking again, trying to quell the noisy beating of her heart when he immediately followed her. It was obvious that he didn't intend to let her out of his sight, so she decided that it would be best if she accepted that. There was no point trying to fight the inevitable when she might need her strength for more important battles.

The traffic congestion eased after a little while. This part of

London was in a state of limbo, she always thought, not quite fashionable but not totally run-down. However, from the look of disdain on Felipe's handsome face as he studied the long row of Victorian terraced houses, it could have been a slum.

He frowned when she stopped outside one of the houses and rang the bell. 'This is where my brother's son spends his days? Surely you could have found somewhere more suitable, a nursery where he would be properly cared for?'

'Josh is very happy here,' she said shortly, stung by the criticism. 'Doreen—that's the childminder—is marvellous with all the children; she loves them as if they were her own. Anyway, I can't afford a nursery place for him. It costs a fortune in London to put a child into a private nursery.'

She realised her mistake the moment she saw his mouth thin into that tight line she was starting to recognise only too well. She was already preparing herself for the next onslaught before he spoke, but nothing could stem the quiver that ran through her when she heard the biting contempt in his voice.

'But my brother left you a considerable sum, didn't he? You were named in his will as the sole beneficiary of his estate. *Sí?*'

'Yes.' She rang the bell a second time, praying that Doreen would answer it soon. She didn't know how she could explain what had happened to the money Antonio had left without giving everything away.

Tara had received most of it as her final payment for having Josh. The little bit that had been left over had been swallowed up by bills in the first few months when she'd been unable to work because she had been looking after the baby. She could account for every single penny if she had to, but it would mean her admitting that she wasn't Josh's real mother and that was something she desperately wanted to avoid.

'So was it too much to expect that you might spend some of that money on making sure that Antonio's son was properly cared for? Did it never cross your mind that you had no right to spend it all on yourself?'

She could hear the anger in his voice and her heart ran wild as she struggled to explain without telling him the truth. 'There were expenses—'

'Expenses? Come, Miss Williams, you must have been enjoying a very lavish lifestyle if you managed to spend all that money in less than a year!' he shot back, glaring at her.

'It wasn't like that. You don't understand,' she said desperately, hurt beyond belief by the way he was looking at her. 'I didn't spend—'

The door suddenly opened and she stopped when Doreen appeared, holding Josh. Becky automatically reached out and took the child as he lunged towards her. She snuggled him close, breathing in his wonderful baby smell while she tried to calm down.

If Doreen hadn't opened the door then she would have blurted it all out and told him that nearly every penny of Antonio's inheritance had gone on buying his son. How would Felipe feel about that? Would he blame her for what had happened because it had been her idea?

Felipe felt his anger disappear the moment he looked at the baby in Rebecca's arms.

The little boy was the image of Antonio!

From his shiny black curls to his chubby little feet, he was a miniature replica of his father. In that instant any doubts he'd had about the child's parentage disappeared. This was Antonio's son, his own flesh and blood.

He wasn't aware of what he was doing as he held out his arms. The little boy gurgled happily as Rebecca silently handed him over. He could feel the weight of the child's sturdy little body in his arms and had to make a conscious effort not to hold him too tightly.

He wanted to press him to his heart and keep him there, pretend, even if it was only for a moment, that he had Antonio back and that he could keep him safe from harm. It was all he had ever wanted to do and he had failed, but he wouldn't fail this child, his brother's son.

It was a moment which Felipe knew he would remember all his life, a moment of such pain and such joy that he found it hard to comprehend what he was feeling. It was as though all of a sudden a key had turned and the door to his heart had been flung wide open. It was a relief when the baby suddenly grabbed a handful of his hair and tugged it hard, because he wasn't used to dealing with so much emotion.

A smile tugged at the corners of Felipe's mouth as he gently unfurled the baby's fingers. 'I shall have no hair left if you keep that up, young man,' he told him in Spanish. 'Your uncle will be bald.'

'He's a devil for pulling your hair,' Becky said softly. 'It's a wonder I'm not bald as well the way he tugs my hair.'

Felipe's black brows rose in surprise. 'You speak Spanish?'

'Yes. I'm not very fluent, but I can get by.' She gave him a sad little smile that made his heart ache all over again. 'Antonio offered to give me Spanish lessons in exchange for a favour I did him. That's how we became friends.'

She looked at the baby and sighed. 'I've tried to keep it up so that I can teach Josh when he's old enough. It seemed important that he should be able to speak his father's language.'

Felipe was deeply moved, so much so that he didn't dare show how much it had affected him. He passed the baby back to her, trying to put what he had learned into context. It was probably just some wonderful story that she had dreamed up to impress him…

Only he didn't believe that.

He went back down the steps while she had a final word with the childminder. It was obvious that the woman was asking who he was, but he didn't feel inclined to join in the conversation. He needed to clear his mind so that he could focus on what he intended to do.

Josh was Antonio's son. There wasn't any doubt in his mind about that. Obviously, he would need to take that into account before he made any decisions.

He took a deep breath but the tension that had been building inside him all day was suddenly worse than ever. Rebecca was the child's mother. He would need to take account of that as well.

Doreen had been intrigued to learn that Felipe was Josh's uncle. Becky kept trying to edge away but the woman kept asking her more questions. Becky glanced over her shoulder and sighed when she saw Felipe standing by the kerb.

It was obvious that he was impatient to leave, even though he was making an effort not to show it. However, the number of times Felipe had needed to wait for anyone had to be few and far between. He was the kind of man who was accustomed to people jumping to obey his every command.

The thought was a little disquieting, but Becky refused to let him see how on edge she felt as she finally took her leave of the childminder. Josh was gurgling away, trying to tell her what he had done during the day. They usually played a game on the way home: she asked him questions about his day and pretended she understood what he was saying to her. However, that day she felt far too self-conscious with Felipe being there. It would hardly improve his opinion of her to know that she held in-depth conversations with a nine-month-old baby!

'What happens now? Do you usually take Josh straight home?'

She jumped when he spoke, wondering why she should be the least bit worried about what he thought of her. Felipe's views on her as a person had been expounded in graphic detail the day before and she doubted if anything would improve his opinion.

It was a painful thought so she focused on the question instead because it was easier. 'Yes. He's had his supper at Doreen's so he just needs a bath and a cuddle, then it will be time for him to go to bed.'

'It appears that you spend very little time with him. Surely it can't be good for a child this young to spend so much time away from his mother?'

She shrugged, not wanting him to guess that the thought had troubled her often during the past few months. 'He seems perfectly happy. And I need to work.'

'Because of the money?'

'Yes,' she snapped, disliking his tone. It hurt to know that he believed she was capable of such massive self-indulgence but, short of telling him the truth about the money, there was nothing she could do.

She quickened her pace, not bothering to check if he was keeping up as they made their way along the street. She lived just a short walk away from the childminder's house so it took them barely five minutes to reach her flat. She stopped on the step, juggling a wriggling Josh in her arms while she hunted her key out of her bag.

'I'll take him.'

Felipe lifted the baby out of her arms without giving her a chance to reply. Becky's mouth thinned because it seemed yet another example of his high-handed attitude. What made it worse was the fact that Josh was obviously delighted to have his uncle holding him.

The baby's chuckles accompanied them as they made their way up the three flights of stairs to the top floor. She rented the attic flat and had always felt quite proud of the fact that she'd transformed a rather dingy space into a place of colour and light. Now, as she slid her key into the lock, she found herself wondering what Felipe would think of her home. Recalling the elegance of the Clinica Valdez, she doubted if his opinion would be all that favourable.

'Put Josh in his play-pen,' she instructed as she let them into the tiny hall. She tossed her bag onto the small table she'd spent so much time lovingly restoring and slipped off her coat. 'It's through there, in the sitting-room.'

Felipe didn't say anything as he carried the child into the adjoining room. Becky hung her coat on a peg then followed him. She paused in the doorway and watched him looking around, wondering what he would think of the place.

She'd worked so hard scraping the walls to get rid of the hideous paper the previous tenants had hung, but she'd been really pleased with the results. At this time of the day, when the evening sun was streaming in through the skylight, the whole room seemed to glow, the rich, golden yellow paint she had chosen for the walls reflecting the light.

The furniture was a mismatched assortment bought from the local flea market, but she'd spent hours polishing the scratches out of the coffee-table and sewing new mossy-green covers for the old sofa.

An area rug in faded green and gold—another flea-market find—made a small oasis in the centre of the floor and set off the richness of the polished wooden floorboards. She had done everything she could to make a pleasant home for herself and Josh, but would Felipe realise how much effort and love she'd put into it?

'This is charming. The colour of the walls, the sun-light…everything.' He smiled and she felt instantly warmed when she saw the approval in his eyes.

'Thank you,' she said softly, looking around. 'I wanted it to be a real home for Josh, so it seemed worth it.'

'Ah, I see. You had someone to decorate for you?' He shot another assessing look around the room. 'I should have realised. No wonder you have managed to spend so much money. It is extremely costly, hiring a good interior designer. *Sí?*'

'No! I didn't hire anyone. I did it all myself. I meant that it had been worth all the effort!'

She took a deep breath when she saw Josh's lower lip start to wobble when he heard her raised voice. It wasn't fair to upset him because Felipe was set on believing the worst about her. 'I suggest we stick to what needs to be said, Dr Valdez. Trying to be polite to one another is pointless.'

'Of course. I am in full agreement with you, Rebecca.'

He carefully put Josh into the play-pen and handed him some soft plastic blocks before he looked at her again. 'I hope you don't mind if I call you Rebecca. After all, we are virtually family so it seems silly to continue being so formal. And you must call me Felipe, of course.'

'My friends call me Becky,' she said automatically. She looked up when he laughed, feeling her stomach churn when she saw the disdain on his face.

'I doubt if you and I will ever be friends, Rebecca. I think that is asking too much of both of us.'

He pinned her with a cool stare that seemed to draw out what little warmth she had in her body. 'I am prepared to tolerate you purely and simply because you are the mother of my brother's child. And for Antonio's sake I am also prepared to treat you with a degree of civility. However, given the choice, I would have nothing whatsoever to do with you. Is that clear?'

'Perfectly clear, Felipe,' she replied, praying that he couldn't hear the hurt in her voice.

Becky turned away, fighting to control the rush of tears that threatened her. She wouldn't break down again. She wouldn't give him the satisfaction of knowing that he'd hurt her. And yet there was something in his voice when he continued that told her he had guessed and that it wasn't satisfaction he was feeling, oddly enough. It threw her into total confusion to hear that note of regret in his voice so that it was a moment before she realised what he had said.

'When *we* go to Mallorca? What do you mean?' she demanded incredulously.

'It is quite simple, Rebecca. Antonio's son should be brought up in the country of his father's birth. He deserves better than the life you can give him here. That is why you and Josh will be moving to Mallorca as soon as I can make all the necessary arrangements.'

He smiled sardonically when she gasped. 'And as an inducement, which I know you won't be able to resist, I am prepared to give you however much money you want. How much were you planning on asking me for when you came to see me yesterday?'

'Twenty thousand pounds,' she murmured, unable to lie because she was so shocked. He couldn't honestly believe that she would agree to uproot herself and Josh and move to another country to live. It was ridiculous.

'So little?' His black brows rose steeply. 'I expected you to demand a much larger sum than that, but if you are happy with that amount then so be it. However, I must warn you, Rebecca, that this will be the one and only time that I shall give you any money. From now on you will need to earn your living.'

'Earn my living,' she repeated dully. She took a deep breath, hoping it would clear her head. Everything seemed to be whirling around so that it was difficult to think. 'I do that already. I earn my living by working at the hospital.'

'*Claro que sí!* Of course, and how fortunate that you have such marketable skills at your disposal.' Felipe smiled and she shivered when she saw the chill in his brown eyes.

'There will be a job waiting for you at the Clinica Valdez as soon as you move to Mallorca. How well everything is working out for you, Rebecca. *Sí?*'

CHAPTER FOUR

FELIPE held his smile but it was an effort. Rebecca was staring at him and it was obvious how shocked she was. It didn't make him feel good to know that he was responsible for that expression of horror on her face so that it was a relief when Josh suddenly started to wail.

Bending, he lifted the child out of the play-pen and handed him to her. 'Perhaps he is tired.'

'Yes.'

Her voice was so low that he had difficulty hearing the single word, but he refused to let himself dwell on how upset she appeared to be. He had to remember that this woman was capable of anything if it meant that she could get her own way. Hadn't she deceived Antonio, tricked him into leaving her all that money, hastened his death by encouraging him to refuse further treatment?

Anger rose swiftly inside him, but he managed to curb it in case he frightened the child. The baby was the innocent victim of Rebecca's scheming and he wouldn't do anything to harm Josh, although that didn't mean he wouldn't get to the bottom of what had gone on. Something told him that there was still a lot about this situation that he hadn't been told.

Felipe sat down on the sofa as Rebecca carried the baby from the room. The sun was streaming through the skylight and he closed his eyes as he settled back against the cushions. He could hear the murmur of her voice as she spoke to the baby, the sound of water running as she filled the bath. They were such ordinary, everyday sounds and yet they filled him with a sense of unreality. He had never imagined when he had got on the plane that morning that this would happen.

He got up, suddenly too on edge to sit still. He prowled

51

around the room, picking up a book from the coffee-table and
putting it down again, taking an ornament off the shelf then
replacing it. His hand brushed against a photograph which had
been propped against a small glass vase, and he sighed when
it fell to the floor.

He picked it up and felt his heart ache when he realised that
it was a picture of Antonio holding Josh. If Rebecca hadn't
told him that story about how his brother had loved to sit holding the baby, he might not have recognised Antonio. He was
a doctor and he'd seen the devastation that cancer could cause
many times, but it was hard to believe that this gaunt-faced
man was the brother whom he had loved and cared for most
of his adult life.

'That was taken two days before he died.'

He looked round when he realised that Rebecca had come
back into the room. He felt so choked with emotion that it was
impossible to reply, and she seemed to understand that. A fris-
son raced through him because he had never imagined that a
woman like her would be capable of such sensitivity.

'I always think Antonio looks so peaceful in that photo.
That's why I like to keep it where I can see it.'

She came and stood beside him and he could smell the scent
of baby soap and talc that clung to her skin. Reaching out, she
ran her finger over the picture and there was something almost
heartbreakingly sad about the way she let it linger on his
brother's smiling face.

'It's his smile, I think. He looks like a man who's been given
the one thing he wanted most.'

Felipe cleared his throat but it was an effort to rid his voice
of all the emotion he could feel welling inside him. 'You mean
Josh?'

'Yes. Having Josh was the most important thing that could
have happened to Antonio. It made everything else bearable.'

He heard the fervour in her voice and frowned. It was obviously important to her that he should believe that, and he
couldn't understand why. He'd accepted that the thought of the

baby had helped Antonio through those last, difficult days so why did Rebecca feel it was necessary to stress that to him?

Once again he had the feeling that there was a lot he didn't understand, but he also knew that he would have to bide his time. She would only tell him what she wanted him to know. Maybe it would help if he tried to win her confidence, although the thought wasn't wholly a comfortable one. Becoming the confidant of this woman wasn't a role he'd planned on playing.

'Did you look after Antonio or did he have someone else to take care of him?' he said, deliberately keeping his tone free from any hint of criticism.

It was something which had bothered him many times; he had lain awake wondering if Antonio had been well cared for after he'd left hospital.

'Both. I took care of his day-to-day needs—washing, feeding and so on—and the hospital arranged for the Macmillan nurses to visit him each day. They were absolutely marvellous. They are specialist nurses who deal with the care of the terminally ill and they were able to adjust Antonio's drugs regime as and when necessary.'

She moved away and sat on the sofa, tilting back her head and closing her eyes just as Felipe had done a short time before. The comparison made his skin prickle, as though it had forged a bond between them.

He cleared his throat again, deeply disturbed by the idea that he and Rebecca might have anything in common. 'If Antonio had been persuaded to stay in hospital, he would not have needed to be treated by them.'

'No, he wouldn't.' A smile curled her mouth, although she didn't open her eyes. 'I lost count of the number of times I tried explaining that to him, but he wouldn't listen. And in the end he was proved right.'

'Right? How can you say that?' Anger flowed through him and he glared at her even though she couldn't see his expression. 'My brother might have lived another six months if he'd remained in hospital!'

'Yes, he might have done. But you're a doctor and you must

have some experience of dealing with patients with terminal
cancer. There comes a point when the decision has to be made
either to prolong life or to try and improve its quality.'

Her eyes suddenly opened and Felipe was surprised when he
saw the assurance they held. 'Antonio refused to undergo any
more treatment because it made him feel so ill. He thought it
all through and weighed up what he was doing. His consultant
had told him that there was no possibility of them curing him—
they were simply trying to buy him extra time. He decided that
he preferred quality to quantity.'

It made sense. In the logical part of his mind, Felipe knew
that, but he couldn't and wouldn't accept that *she* hadn't been
the one to influence his brother for her own ends.

'And the fact that Antonio's decision fitted in so perfectly
with your plans was just a bonus?' he said acidly.

'I didn't try to influence Antonio in any way,' she stated,
and there was something about her calmness and lack of emotion that made it impossible to dispute what she had said.

Felipe felt his head whirl as once again he was forced to
reassess his opinion of her. Rebecca hadn't persuaded Antonio
to refuse treatment. The decision had been his brother's. Was
it the shock of realising that which filled him with such relief?

He pushed that thought to the back of his mind as Rebecca
got up and went to the old-fashioned bureau by the door.
Opening one of the drawers, she took out a wad of photographs
and handed them to him.

'These are all of Antonio, taken shortly after he found out
about Josh right up till the week he died.' She gave a husky
laugh. 'He used to groan every time I appeared with the cam-
era, but it seemed important that Josh should have some idea
what his father looked like in years to come.'

Felipe sat down because his legs suddenly felt too weak to
hold him. He flicked through the pictures then went back to
the beginning and studied them more slowly. He could see the
deterioration in his brother's appearance as the months had
passed, and yet the one thing that struck him was that even

though his health had been failing, Antonio had looked increasingly serene.

'Did he not feel bitter about what was happening?' he asked, staring at the pictures one after the other.

'Oh, yes, at first he did. He was very bitter—and angry, too. Who wouldn't be? He was twenty-five and going to die.' She sighed. 'We spent night after night talking it all through, trying to make sense of it, but you can't rationalise something like that, can you? In the end, Antonio realised that himself.'

'Was he working at the time—when he found out that he was ill, I mean?' he asked, wondering if he would have had the strength of mind to cope. It shook him that his brother— the brother he had always taken care of—had dealt with his illness with such equanimity because Felipe himself wasn't sure if he could have managed that.

'Yes, and he continued working right up until a couple of months before he died.'

She came and sat beside him on the sofa and he felt a tremor run through his body when she leant over to look at the photographs. All of a sudden he was so deeply aware of her that he could barely breathe. He could feel the warmth of her arm next to his, the slight pressure of her hip as she settled herself more comfortably on the seat. He had to make a conscious effort to drag some air into his lungs, yet he still felt strangely breathless after he had done so.

'He worked as a session musician at one of the clubs not far from here. He played guitar, as you know, and a couple of nights they gave him a solo spot when Tara wasn't singing.'

'Tara?' he queried automatically, forcing himself to concentrate when she carried on speaking. He felt a sharp stab of pain spear him. It grieved him to realise how far apart he and Antonio had drifted. He'd had no idea that his brother had been earning his living through his music. It had been Antonio's dream, of course, the only thing he had ever wanted to do and the cause of that dreadful argument they'd had.

Antonio had wanted to be a musician and he had tried to persuade him to choose a different career, something that would be more lucrative and stable. How very pointless it all seemed now.

Felipe looked up when he realised that Rebecca hadn't answered, and felt his heart turn over when he saw the expression on her face. He couldn't recall ever seeing anyone who looked as stricken as she did at that moment.

He took another deep breath but his voice sounded strained when it emerged. Maybe he was mistaken, but he had a gut feeling that her answer might hold the key to what had really gone on.

'Who is Tara? And what was her relationship to my brother?'

Becky could feel her pulse racing. She couldn't believe she had allowed Tara's name to slip out!

She summoned a smile but she knew how difficult it was going to be to extricate herself from this mess. Felipe was obviously suspicious and she had to be extremely careful what she said.

'Tara Lewis. She sings at the club where Antonio worked. Antonio went out with her for a time when he first arrived in London.' She shrugged. 'We met after he and Tara had split up so that's all I can tell you, I'm afraid.'

She stood up, gathering together the photographs to give herself a breathing space, but her heart was racing. Had Felipe believed her?

She shot him a wary glance and bit her lip when she saw the frown on his handsome face. Although there was a strong resemblance between him and Antonio, it was far more difficult to tell what Felipe was thinking. She took rapid stock of the thin-lipped, oddly sensual mouth, the long straight nose with its slightly flaring nostrils and the angular cheekbones in the hope that it might help if she took note of the similarities between the two men.

There definitely was a strong family likeness, although Felipe's features were more austere than Antonio's. His hair was just as thick and black as Antonio's had been when she'd met him, but whereas Antonio had worn his long, Felipe's was cut very short, the crisp strands lying neatly against his well-shaped head.

Once again that day he was wearing a suit, and again the fine black cloth was tailored to perfection. His white shirt looked as fresh as when he must have put it on that morning and his burgundy silk tie was perfectly knotted.

Antonio hadn't even possessed a suit to her knowledge. She certainly hadn't seen him wearing one. Jeans and a shirt had been his usual attire and she couldn't remember him ever wearing anything else.

His style had been casual, easygoing, a world removed from the sophisticated face Felipe presented to the world. Maybe she should take that as a warning. It would be a mistake to underestimate what Felipe was capable of by comparing him to his brother.

'How long exactly were you and my brother together?'

Becky started nervously when he spoke and some of the photographs shot out of her hands and fell onto the floor. Bending, she scooped them into a pile then jumped again when Felipe handed her one that had slid under the sofa.

'Thank you,' she said quietly, walking to the bureau. She placed the photos back in the drawer then turned to face him, praying that he couldn't tell how difficult this was for her. It would be so easy to make another slip. The last thing she wanted was for him to start adding everything up and working out that she couldn't possibly be Josh's mother.

'I really can't see where this is leading. What difference does it make how long Antonio and I were together? We had Josh, didn't we?'

'So you did, and that should tell me everything I need to know.'

He stood up abruptly and she had to physically stop herself backing away when he came towards her. 'After all, it's the child who is my main concern now, my brother's son. It is his future I intend to focus on.'

'Of course. But what you said about us moving to Mallorca…well, you do realise that it is out of the question?'

She summoned a smile but the way he was looking at her wasn't reassuring. 'My life is here in England and I have no intention of uprooting myself and Josh.'

'I don't see that you have any choice, Rebecca, not if you want to keep your son.'

'What do you mean?' she demanded, feeling the blood starting to drum in her temples again.

'Simply that I'm sure, with the right lawyers at my disposal, I could make a very good case if I decided to sue for custody of the child.'

He smiled but there wasn't a hint of warmth in his eyes as they skimmed her face. 'Once I point out to the judge that you only had the baby so that it would give you a certain... *leverage* over my brother then I'm sure he would find in my favour.

'You had Josh purely and simply for the money, didn't you, Rebecca? It's taken a little time for everything to slot into place, but I know that I'm right. Antonio bought himself a son. It's as simple as that.'

Felipe watched the guilty colour sweep up her face and knew that he was right. Rebecca had had the baby as a means to extract money from his brother.

It was an effort to hide his disgust but he knew that it would be giving her an advantage if he let her see how much it had upset him to finally learn the truth. He had to pretend that it made no difference, but he knew in his heart that it did.

He felt deeply and bitterly disappointed, and the fact that he could feel such an emotion about this woman dismayed him. He'd known all along what she was like, so why should he feel upset because he had been proved right?

Suddenly, he knew that he couldn't take any more. He turned and strode to the door, barely pausing when she called out 'Wait!' in a quavery little voice. He turned to look at her, steeling himself when he saw the total absence of colour in her face.

'Yes?'

'What do you intend to do... about Josh, I mean?'

'That depends on what you decide to do, Rebecca.' He

shrugged, striving for a nonchalance he wished he felt. 'I am not prepared to leave my brother's son here in England with you. It's as simple as that.'

'But I have a job here, a home, friends,' she protested.

'You will have a job and a home in Mallorca. As for friends—well, that will be up to you, of course. Although, naturally, I would take a poor view of you becoming involved with anyone unsuitable. It might be best if you concentrated on being a mother for a while and forgot about your love life.'

He saw her open her mouth then shut it again, and found himself wondering what she'd been going to say before she had thought better of it. Had she been about to claim to him that her only concern *was* her child?

Felipe felt a bitter laugh welling inside him and turned so that Rebecca couldn't see his expression. Women like her were magnets to men, and it wouldn't be long before she found someone else to take Antonio's place, if she hadn't already done so, of course.

The thought stung far more than it should, but he gave no sign of it as he walked along the hall. He let himself out of the flat and in deference to the sleeping child didn't slam the door behind him as he felt like doing. The encounter had left a sour taste in his mouth, a feeling of heaviness in his heart. As he strode down the stairs Felipe inwardly cursed.

Damn Rebecca Williams and her scheming and conniving, her trickery and treachery. Damn her for being everything he had thought she would be, and worse!

Becky heard the door closing and only then did she let herself breathe. Her lungs were burning from the lack of oxygen but Felipe's accusation had stolen her ability to perform such a rudimentary task. He had been right in a way and yet so horribly wrong that it was the bitterest kind of irony. It hadn't been her who had sold her baby but Tara!

She made herself take another deep breath in the hope that it would ease the pain she felt. Maybe it was silly to get upset, but it hurt to know that he believed her capable of such a dreadful thing. However, Felipe's views on her really weren't the most pressing issue at the moment. She had to decide what she intended to do.

The choice appeared to be perfectly simple—she could agree to Felipe's demands and move to Mallorca with Josh, and by so doing she had would obtain the money she needed to pay Tara, or she could refuse and end up with nothing. She didn't doubt that Tara would carry out her threat to take her to court— and even if she didn't, Felipe would.

A bitter smile curled her mouth. It didn't seem like much of a choice after all.

'What did you say?'

'I said that I'm moving to Mallorca at the end of the month.' Becky summoned a smile but it was hard to maintain an out- ward show of happiness when her heart felt like lead.

She had spent a sleepless night, trying to find another solu- tion to her problems, but the answer kept coming out the same no matter which way she approached it. If she moved to Mallorca she would be able to pay off Tara. It would also mean that she could get Josh out of London because she wasn't fool- ish enough to believe that Tara wouldn't demand more money at some point in the future. Moving to Mallorca would solve that problem, although it was bound to create others.

Her heart lurched at the thought of what Felipe might do if he found out the truth—that she wasn't Josh's real mother— but she couldn't worry about that now. She had to deal with this a step at a time, and the first step was to inform her col- leagues of her decision, as she was in the process of doing.

'I don't know what to say... I mean it's all rather sudden, isn't it, Becky?' Simon Montague's pleasant face filled with concern. They were in the staff canteen, having their lunch, and he leant forward so that the people at the next table couldn't hear him. 'You're not in any kind of trouble, are you?'

'Of course not! Why on earth do you think that?' She tried to laugh but it sounded too forced to be convincing and she saw Simon frown.

'Because nobody makes a rush decision like this about their

future.' He shook his head when she went to speak. 'No, don't, Becky. I can tell you're going to deny it, but I know I'm right. Karen told me about Josh's uncle turning up yesterday and how upset you appeared to be. Has this anything to do with him?'

'No, of course not,' she began, then sighed when she saw the look he gave her. 'Well, yes, I suppose it has. Felipe told me that he would like to spend more time with Josh,' she explained, skating over the facts to make them more palatable. 'It was his idea that we should move to Mallorca and I just thought it would be good for all of us.'

'He could fly over here and see him,' Simon said bluntly. 'It only takes three hours so it's not as though he would need to travel from one side of the globe to the other. It takes me longer when I go up to Scotland to visit my family.'

'I know,' she agreed, wishing that she'd given a bit more thought to what she intended to tell everyone. 'But it wouldn't be the same as seeing Josh on a daily basis, would it? You know how fast children grow up and—'

'And I've never heard such a cock-and-bull story in my life!' Simon's face was almost as red as his hair as he leant across the table and gripped her hand. 'This guy, Valdez, is putting pressure on you, isn't he, Becky? What's he threatening to do, try and get custody of Josh? He sounds very possessive.'

Becky shivered. She couldn't help wondering if Simon was right. Did Felipe feel possessive about Josh? The fact that the baby was his nephew was bound to create a tie between them, but might he feel that it was his duty to take over the role Antonio would have played in the little boy's life? Did Felipe see himself as a substitute father perhaps?

The thought was deeply disquieting because it made her see just how tenuous her position was. If Felipe ever found out that she wasn't Josh's real mother, he could order her out of the child's life. The thought of the little boy growing up without her was more than she could bear and tears filled her eyes.

'Oh, hell! I didn't mean to scare you, Becky. Take no notice of me. There isn't a court in the world who would take a child away from its mother and hand him over to a total stranger.'

Simon grimaced as he gave her fingers a reassuring squeeze. 'I'm just letting my imagination run away with me because it was such a shock to hear that you'll be leaving. I'm really going to miss you, you know?'

'And I'm going to miss you, too, Simon, really I am.' She dashed the tears from her eyes and summoned a smile. The urge to tell him the whole sorry story was very strong, but she knew in her heart that she couldn't burden him with it. Simon was a good friend, but it wouldn't be fair to expect him to solve her problems.

'Who's going to make sure I get my daily ration of chocolate biscuits?' she teased, with an attempt at levity.

'Cupboard love! So that's it. Here I was thinking that you found me irresistible and all you're really after is the bickies I keep bringing you.' He rolled his eyes comically, but she wasn't blind to the disappointment they held. 'It's the story of my life!'

'I can't help it if I have a sweet tooth.'

Becky swallowed a sigh because she couldn't help wishing that her life was less complicated. If it had been, there would be nothing to stop her going out with Simon. He had asked her often enough, but she had always found some excuse to turn him down. She was fond of him but not really attracted to him. She had always been more attracted to dark-haired men like Antonio...

She bit her lip as an image sprang to mind, because it wasn't Antonio's face she had conjured up but Felipe's. It was as though Felipe had suddenly supplanted Antonio in her thoughts. The idea made her tremble and she saw Simon look at her in alarm.

'Are you OK?'

'Fine. Just a bit worn out with everything that's been happening recently.'

'It can't have been an easy decision to make, Becky. I don't think I'd fancy just upping and leaving as you're planning on doing, but, then, I don't have a child to consider.' He gave her a quick smile. 'You're doing this for Josh, aren't you?'

'Yes.' She took a steadying breath. It would serve no purpose to worry about why she had thought of Felipe instead of Antonio when there were more important matters to consider.

'I believe this is the right thing for Josh,' she said firmly, trying to inject a degree of certainty into her voice. It obviously worked because Simon nodded in agreement.

'Then I hope it works out for you, Becky, really I do.'

'Thank you,' she said, touched by his obvious sincerity.

They changed the subject after that, but it had helped her put everything into perspective. Even though she didn't like the idea of moving to Mallorca and being forced to live in such close to proximity to Felipe, it would mean that Josh would be safe. Tara wouldn't be able to find them there and she would no longer have to worry about her threats.

Simon had to leave shortly afterwards so Becky finished her lunch and went out onto the terrace for a few minutes before she returned to the ward. It was a particularly clear day and the view over the city was superb. She could see Big Ben and the Houses of Parliament, and the silvery curve of the London Eye shimmering in the sunshine.

She had lived in London for most of her adult life and was used to the sights, but that day she saw them with a fresh eye. Soon there would be new sights to see, a new way of life to get used to. It would be a big change when she moved to Mallorca but she would cope. She really would. For Josh's sake she would make the adjustment.

Maybe Felipe believed that he had forced her hand but it no longer felt that way. The decision was hers, not his, and as long as she stopped him finding out the truth about Josh, she could continue making decisions about the child's future. Felipe Valdez was the baby's uncle, not his father. As long as he understood what his role was, they should get along fine.

The view suddenly swam before her eyes. *Should*, not *would*, because there weren't any guarantees.

CHAPTER FIVE

FELIPE was feeling decidedly out of sorts by the time lunchtime arrived. He phoned room service and ordered a plate of sandwiches and a pot of coffee because he knew that he should eat something. He'd spent a sleepless night going over everything that had happened, examining each and every word Rebecca had said, but he still couldn't rid himself of the nagging feeling that he was missing something.

He went to the window, resting his head tiredly against the glass as he looked out. His room overlooked one of the parks and he could see dozens of people taking advantage of the fine weather. The triple glazing meant that there was no sound coming into the room from outside and it added a sense of unreality to the scene to be able to watch people talking and not hear what they were saying.

He turned away from the view, suddenly impatient with himself. He should be thinking about what Rebecca intended to do instead of worrying about the conversations of a bunch of strangers. Would she agree to his demands to move to Mallorca, or would she refuse?

It would be marvellous to think that he had the power to make her do what he wanted, but the truth was that he didn't. It was the uncertainty that was causing him such anguish, the fear that he might not be able to do anything for Antonio's son after all. He didn't think he could bear it if he failed in this, as he had failed to look after his brother.

The phone suddenly rang and he hurried towards it then cursed when at the same moment there was a knock on the door. Snatching the receiver from its rest, he rapped out, *'Un momento, por favor!'* Then went to let in the waiter who had brought his lunch.

Felipe tipped the man, and probably too generously from the expression of delight on his face, as he hurriedly left. But money was the least of his concerns even though it could be the deciding factor for Rebecca. If her need for money was great enough, surely she would do as he wanted?

His mouth thinned as he picked up the receiver again. She had used Antonio's child as a commercial venture and it sickened him to know that she was capable of such a thing. It was little wonder that he felt his stomach churn when he recognised her voice on the other end of the line, he told himself. It certainly couldn't be pleasure that had caused it to react like that.

'It's Rebecca. I wonder if I could have a word with you tonight after work?'

'Of course,' he agreed, deliberately removing any trace of emotion from his voice because he didn't want her to guess there was anything wrong. He couldn't explain it, but he felt that it would give her an advantage to know that she possessed this power to upset him. 'What time would be convenient for you?'

'Straight after I leave work would be best. I should finish around six so maybe I could meet you in that bar you mentioned yesterday.'

He heard her take a quick breath and had a sudden, vivid image of her at the other end of the phone line. There would be a tiny frown on her face as she waited to hear what he would say, a hint of uncertainty in her huge grey eyes as she stood there, wondering if he would agree…

He drove the image from his mind, but it unnerved him just how quickly he had managed to conjure up a picture of her. 'That will be fine. Six o'clock it is.'

'Thank you. I…I promise that I won't keep you very long.'

She put down the phone without saying anything else, and after a moment Felipe hung up as well. He went and poured himself a cup of coffee, but all the time he was doing so he kept hearing her voice inside his head, and the hairs on his arms pricked as he recalled its sweetness. All of a sudden, he knew that he couldn't wait for the allotted time to arrive when

he would see her again, and the thought scared him because
he couldn't afford to feel like this where she was concerned.

Rebecca Williams was a scheming, mercenary gold-digger.
He made himself repeat the litany, but it seemed to have lost
its power for some reason. They were just words now, words
that didn't seem to mean very much.

'Let's drop the head of the bed and see if we can get her
pressure back up.'

Becky glanced round, immediately taking note of the panic
on Debbie Rothwell's face. It was obvious that the trainee
wasn't coping well with this latest emergency so she decided
that it would be best if she got her out of the way.

'Debbie, go to the office and ask the switchboard to page
James Watts. I don't like the look of what's happening and I
think we need him here stat.'

Debbie made no attempt to hide her relief as she hurried
away. Becky sighed as she turned back to the patient. It was
becoming increasingly obvious that Debbie didn't have what it
took to work in the IC unit. It wasn't always easy to maintain
one's composure, but it was vital when faced with an emergency such as the one they had to deal with at the moment.

The patient, an eight-year-old girl called Rosie Stokes, had
been transferred to the unit from a hospital in their catchment
area a short time before. Rosie had been involved in a car crash
on her way to school that morning and had suffered a serious
head injury. She'd needed an operation to relieve the pressure
on her brain but, according to the notes that accompanied her,
everything had gone according to plan.

Now, however, she was showing signs of shock and acute
kidney failure, and Becky couldn't understand what had gone
wrong. The child should have been closely monitored from the
time she'd left Theatre to prevent something like this happening.

There had been no bed available in the IC unit that morning,
which was why Rosie had been kept at the other hospital until

one had become free that afternoon. But even without IC care, there were basic procedures that should have been carried out.

'How many mils of urine has she passed since she was admitted?' she asked, glancing at Karen.

Karen checked the plastic bag at the end of the child's bed and shook her head. 'Zero. The bag's empty.'

'This can't just have happened!' Becky exclaimed, checking the monitor readings. Rosie's blood pressure was still falling so she quickly adjusted the drip. 'Even with acute kidney failure there are warning signs, so why weren't they picked up before? How long has she been here now?'

Karen checked the admission notes. 'Less than an hour. She was logged in at ten minutes past four. She had been catheterised prior to her op. I checked her bag and assumed they must have changed it before they transferred her to us. It's only a ten-minute drive from St Ada's after all. But now I'm wondering if that really was the case.'

'From the look of things I'd say that there's been no urine output for some time,' Becky observed worriedly. 'I'll order a blood test to check her levels of urea and creatinine. That will tell us if her kidneys have completely shut down. Heaven knows what's caused it to happen because everything was going smoothly, according to her notes.'

'Could it be internal bleeding?' Karen suggested. 'Something they didn't pick up on earlier.'

'It could, but they should have given her a full examination when she was admitted,' she said bluntly.

'I've heard rumours about St Ada's,' Karen said darkly. 'The word is that the standards there have dropped dramatically of late.'

'It used to be a marvellous hospital, too.' Becky sighed as she set about drawing off the small sample of blood. It saddened her to think that the child's life might have been put at risk because of inadequate nursing care. She couldn't help wondering how she would feel if it were Josh lying in the bed. She would want him to have the very best treatment possible, and resolved to do all she could to help poor Rosie through this crisis.

She quickly sealed the vial and labelled it with the patient's details, checking the child's notes to make sure that she had her date of birth correct. Her eye was caught by a note on the top of the page stating that Rosie's blood group was A-positive and her heart sank in dismay.

'Here, grab hold of this.' She thrust the vial into Karen's hands and hurried around the bed to check the unit of blood that was being drip-fed into the girl's arm. It was clearly labelled as B-positive, not A.

'She's been given the wrong blood,' she said, quickly closing the valve in the line. 'That's why her kidneys have failed and she's in shock.'

'Hell's teeth!' Karen exclaimed. 'How on earth did a thing like that happen?'

'Heaven knows,' Becky replied, rapidly detaching the bag from the cannula in the child's arm. She glanced round when she heard footsteps and grimaced when she saw that James Watts had arrived. 'But somehow I don't think that answer is going to satisfy the boss when he finds out. He's going to be furious.'

'Furious and determined to get to the bottom of this.' Karen sighed as she looked at the clock. 'And to think I was hoping that we might get away on time tonight for once. Fat chance of that happening now!'

Neither of them said anything else because James Watts had reached them by then. As Becky drew the consultant aside and explained what had happened, she couldn't help wondering what Felipe would think when she didn't turn up for their meeting. One thing was certain: it wouldn't be anything favourable. So far as Felipe was concerned there was absolutely nothing about her that met with his approval.

It was odd how much that thought hurt.

Felipe checked his watch again. He'd arrived a good ten minutes before the time they had arranged to meet, but it was now almost seven and there was still no sign of Rebecca. He had just made up his mind to leave if she didn't show up in the next five minutes when she came rushing through the door.

'I'm *so* sorry!' she apologised, hurrying to his table. 'We had an emergency and Mr Watts wanted to hear all the ins and outs, and he can be so pedantic at times! I must have told him a hundred times that it had nothing whatsoever to do with us and that it was the staff at St Ada's he needed to speak to, but he's the sort of person who needs everything written out in triplicate...'

She suddenly stopped and he was intrigued to see a wash of colour flow up her face. 'You really don't want to hear all this, do you? I'm sorry that you had to wait, but it was unavoidable, I'm afraid.'

Felipe smiled, wondering why he felt a need to reassure her. Just for a moment Rebecca had forgotten that he was her enemy and had spoken to him without her usual reserve. It had been an intriguing insight into her as a person and he had to admit that his curiosity had been piqued.

'There is nothing to apologise for. I know only too well the pitfalls involved with the career we have chosen.'

He shrugged, watching the rapid play of emotions that crossed her face. She was obviously trying to decide if she could take what he'd said at face value, and he realised how much he wanted her to believe him. He didn't want her to think of him purely as her enemy, funnily enough.

The thought slid into his mind too quickly to stop it so he chose to ignore it instead. Standing, he politely drew out a chair for her to sit down and frowned when she shook her head.

'Look, I'm sorry to be a nuisance but I really can't stay,' she explained. 'I have to collect Josh because he'll be wondering where I am.' She half turned to leave then paused, and he saw her take a quick breath. He knew that she was steeling herself to say something else and the muscles in his stomach clenched in anticipation.

'Would you like to come with me? I know I suggested that

we meet here and it would have been easier if we'd been able to talk on our own, but...'

'Yes.'

He pushed back his chair, seeing her start of surprise at his easy acquiescence. Frankly, he was rather surprised himself because it wasn't like him to change his plans.

He suddenly found himself thinking that he must try to be a little more flexible in the future. He had to learn how to adapt to this situation, although perhaps that wasn't the most reassuring of thoughts in relation to Rebecca Williams. Exactly how adaptable did he intend to be?

'Of course I would like to come with you,' he said politely, refusing to think too hard about such a facile question.

'Oh, well, good. That solves that problem, then,' she said brightly, but he could see that the flush in her cheeks had deepened.

Felipe allowed himself a small smile as he followed her to the door. It was obvious that Rebecca was surprised by the way he'd acted and it was encouraging to know that he was still able to disconcert her. In the past few hours, he'd had the uncomfortable feeling that the balance of power had shifted in her favour and it was a relief to see that he'd been wrong. He needed to control this area of his life as much as the rest of it.

They had just reached the door when a red-haired man came into the bar. Felipe saw Rebecca stiffen as they all stopped. Instinctively, he put his hand under her elbow and he saw the man look at him before he turned to Rebecca and smiled.

'Fancy seeing you here, Becky. I didn't realise this was one of your haunts.'

'It isn't. I'd arranged to meet Felipe here, but it ended up with me being late,' she said quickly.

Felipe saw her glance nervously at him and frowned. It was obvious that Rebecca was uncomfortable about the encounter, but why? Who was this man?

'Aren't you going to introduce me, Rebecca?' he said smoothly.

'Yes, of course.' She sounded flustered as she set about making the introductions. 'Felipe, this is Simon Montague, the senior registrar on the IC unit. Simon, this is Josh's uncle, Dr Felipe Valdez.'

'Oh, I see. That explains it.' Montague smiled but Felipe could see the hostility in his eyes. 'You're the guy who's trying to persuade Becky to move to Mallorca. Do you really believe that it's in her best interests to leave everything she knows and move to a place where she has no friends?'

'I imagine that is for Rebecca to decide,' Felipe said calmly, trying not to let the younger man see that he was annoyed.

No wonder she was on edge! She had obviously discussed her plans with Montague but it was the reason why she had done so that infuriated him. Had she sounded him out to see if he could come up with a better idea perhaps? After all, if Montague could come up with the money she needed, what reason was there to uproot herself? The truth was that there were always options for a woman like her, always another man gullible enough to help her.

The thought angered him even more but he refused to let either of them see how he felt. He turned to Rebecca and smiled, but maybe he wasn't as adept at hiding his feelings as he'd thought, he realised when he saw her frown. It was obvious that she had sensed something was wrong and it bothered him to know that she'd picked up on his mood so easily.

'We should go. Josh will be wondering where you are,' he told her, deliberately blanking out that thought because it wouldn't help.

'Of course.' She gave him the ghost of a smile before she turned to Simon Montague, and Felipe had to steel himself not to react when he heard the entreaty in her voice. 'I'll catch up with you tomorrow, Simon. Promise. Take care, now.'

'You, too, my sweet.'

Montague gave him another hard stare before they left, but Felipe ignored him. He still had hold of Rebecca's arm but he released her as soon as they were outside. The meeting had left him with a bad taste in his mouth and a feeling of dissatisfaction which he knew was a dangerous indulgence.

So what if Rebecca *was* looking for ways and means to avoid having to do as he wanted her to? What if she *was* trying to keep Montague sweet in the hope that he would help her? Surely it was only what he would have expected of her?

'All right, you may as well tell me what's wrong.' She stopped and glared at him, giving him no choice but to stop as well.

Felipe glanced round, feeling uncomfortable when he saw people staring at them. Rebecca had both hands placed on her slender hips and it must have been obvious to anyone who was passing that she was furiously angry.

'I have no idea what you are talking about,' he said shortly.

'Rubbish! That's just a cop-out because you either don't want to or can't answer the question.'

Her grey eyes shot sparks at him. 'You might be able to fool most people with that ice-man routine, but you don't fool me! Something has upset you and I want to know what it is, although why I am even asking is beyond me. Just the fact that I'm still breathing is probably your worst nightmare, isn't it?'

He saw tears well into her eyes as she turned and began hurrying along the street. He went after her, his long legs quickly making up the distance. He put his hand on her arm to stop her, feeling a ripple of raw awareness shoot through him. It was as though he could suddenly *feel* her pain. He had an overwhelming urge to take her in his arms and comfort her, promise that he would never do anything else to hurt her. Maybe they could find some way to compromise. He didn't want to keep fighting with her...

He took a deep breath as Rebecca shrugged off his hand and carried on walking. He felt quite sick as he realised how foolish he was being. How could he ever compromise? How could he ever forget what she'd done? She deserved everything that happened to her because she had brought it all on herself!

Oddly enough, it didn't make him feel better to realise that. By the time they'd collected Josh and arrived at her flat, he was beginning to feel like the lowest form of pond life.

Rebecca hadn't said a word to him all the way home. She'd totally ignored him as she'd chatted to the baby.

Felipe wasn't used to being ignored and it irked him that she seemed able to blank him out like that. He stood to one side while she juggled the baby and the key before opening the front door. It was clear that any offer of help would be rejected.

He followed her up the three flights of stairs and went into the sitting-room when she disappeared into the bathroom with Josh. What made him feel even worse was that it was all done in a silence that said far more than any amount of angry words.

He sank onto the sofa and closed his eyes. He had known all along that Rebecca had the power to manipulate men. He just hadn't realised that he would be as susceptible as all the rest.

'And here comes another bubble... Pop!'

Becky smiled when Josh chortled with laughter. He was obviously enjoying the fact that she'd let him stay in the bath far longer than normal. He was usually tucked up in his cot by now, but the extra playtime had given her a chance to calm down.

It was silly to get upset but it had been obvious what Felipe had been thinking when they'd met Simon. He believed that Simon was the latest in a long string of men who had come and gone in her life. He wouldn't believe her if she told him the truth, that there were no men in her life, so why get upset? She needed a clear head when she laid down the rules that would have to be met before she agreed to move to Mallorca.

'You will both be waterlogged soon. Do you usually let him play for so long?'

She felt her heart bounce against her ribs when she looked round and saw Felipe standing in the doorway. There was a faint smile on his mouth and a softness about his eyes which she hadn't seen before. She found herself thinking how wonderful it would be to have him look at her that way all the time before common sense reasserted itself. Any softening in his attitude was because of Josh, not because of anything she had done.

'Not usually,' she said coolly, trying her best not to let him see how much that thought had upset her. 'I thought he deserved a little treat tonight—didn't you, poppet?'

She went to kiss the top of Josh's damp head and gasped when he suddenly slammed both chubby little fists into the water. A wave of soap suds lapped over the side of the bath and landed in her lap.

Felipe laughed throatily when he saw what had happened. 'It is truly amazing how much mess one small child can make, *sí?*'

'It is.' Becky grabbed a towel from the rack and mopped at her skirt, but the water had soaked right through it. Tossing the towel aside, she pulled a face at the little boy.

'You're a monster, Joshua Valdez! I'm going to splash you back for doing that.'

She gently patted the water and sent a soapy wave cascading over the baby's tummy, much to his delight. He rapidly beat his hands up and down in the water to show his appreciation. Becky groaned as another little tidal wave slopped over the side of the bath and once again landed on her. 'Well, I've only got myself to blame, I suppose.'

'Would you like me to stay here and watch him while you change into some dry clothes?'

She stared at him. 'You?'

A little colour ran up Felipe's cheeks when he heard the surprise in her voice. 'I think I am capable of looking after him for a short while. I assure you that I know all about the dangers of leaving a young child unattended in the bath, so you can trust me not to wander off.'

'I didn't mean that you weren't capable. I just meant that it doesn't really seem your sort of thing.' She shrugged, wishing that she'd simply refused the offer rather than try to explain how she felt about it. 'I mean, how often have you ever bathed a baby?'

'Ah, now, let me see.' He stared at the ceiling and there was an expression of such intense concentration on his face that she found herself holding her breath.

'Twice, I think. Yes, that's right, although I have to confess that one time it wasn't a real baby.'

'Not a real baby?' she parroted, feeling her heart perform the most peculiar manoeuvre when he suddenly smiled at her. It felt as though it had performed a full three-hundred-and-sixty-degree turn, which was a physiological impossibility. However, even knowing that didn't negate the effect it had had so it was an effort to concentrate when he continued.

'No. It was a doll, you see, a very ugly, very pink, rubber doll called Esmeralda.'

His lips twitched when he saw her eyes widen but his voice remained perfectly composed. 'I grew very fond of that doll, in fact. I was quite sad when the time came for us to go our separate ways.'

Becky opened her mouth then shut it again because she wasn't sure what to say in response to such an admission. The thought of Felipe 'growing fond' of a pink, rubber doll was rather too much to take in.

She stared at him, hoping that he would tell her more, wondering why she should want to hear it. Why on earth should she be interested in a crazy story like this? And yet she knew that she was.

He gave her another one of those highly unsettling smiles but this time she was prepared and her heart only managed half a turn not a full one.

'My first job after I qualified was in a maternity unit. I do not wish to be unkind but the sister there was an absolute dragon—there is no other word I can think of to describe her.'

Felipe laughed softly when her mouth twitched. 'I can tell that you understand what I mean, Rebecca. Everything had to be done according to her rules and heaven help any member of staff—nurses or doctors—who failed to meet her exacting standards.'

'I've worked with a few like that over the years,' she admitted. 'So go on, tell me about the doll.'

He leant against the side of the bath, smiling as he watched Josh happily splashing. 'It was one of Sister's strictest rules that everyone who worked in her ward must know how to bathe and dress a baby as well as feed and change it. She didn't trust us with any of her precious babies, of course, so she had purchased the doll especially for this purpose. I shall never forget the sight of grown men sweating as they struggled to put a nappy onto that bundle of pink plastic.'

Becky burst out laughing. 'Oh, I can just picture it! What a wonderful story, Felipe. It's one of those tales that gets better every time you tell it, isn't it?'

'I wouldn't know. It is the first time I have ever told anyone the story.' He shrugged but she saw the uncertainty that had clouded his beautiful eyes. 'I am not sure why I told you just now, to be honest.'

'To convince me that you are capable of looking after Josh for a few minutes,' she said quickly, because she didn't want him to start regretting what he had done.

She stood up, trying to hide how touched she felt because he had chosen to tell her that tale when he had told nobody else. Had he been afraid that people would laugh *at* him and not *with* him if he had told them? she wondered.

She sensed it was so and it just served to make her feel even more confused that he should have confided in her when he'd made no secret of the fact that he didn't like her.

'Right, now that I know you're fully qualified to care for babies, I'll leave you in charge while I find something dry to wear,' she said, adopting a deliberately bright tone because she didn't want him to suspect anything was wrong. 'Just don't blame me if you end up regretting your impulsive offer. This little horror is a dab hand with the water!'

'So I can see.' He smiled, but she could tell that he was still rather puzzled by what he'd done.

Becky headed for the door, knowing that it was pointless dwelling on it. She was just about to leave him to it when a thought suddenly occurred to her and she paused to look back. 'You said that you'd bathed two babies. You've explained about Esmeralda, but what about the other baby? Was it a real one?'

'Oh, yes, it was real.'

He took off his jacket and rolled up his shirtsleeves before he crouched beside the bath. Becky saw him scoop up a handful of water and watched as he let it dribble through his fingers onto Josh's tummy. She wasn't sure how she knew what he was going to say, but all of a sudden her heart began to ache.

'I helped my mother bath Antonio when she brought him home from hospital. He was just three days old and like most fifteen-year-old boys I had never touched a child so small before.'

He looked up and there was a world of pain in his eyes when he looked at her. 'I made a promise on that day that I would always take care of him, but I failed. I wasn't there when he needed me most.'

Becky didn't know what to say. Anything sounded trite in the face of his grief. All the anger she'd felt about the way he had behaved towards her suddenly seemed self-indulgent. Felipe was tormenting himself because he hadn't been able to do anything to help his brother, and yet he had nothing to blame himself for.

She took a deep breath but there was only one thing she could say that might comfort him. 'You're here now and that's what matters. Antonio would be so pleased to know that you're going to take care of his son.'

She didn't wait to hear what he might say as she quickly left the room. She went into her bedroom and sat on the bed, feeling the fear uncoiling inside her. She had just given Felipe permission to play a central role in Josh's life. Although she knew it had been the right thing to do, it still scared her. The more she involved him in Josh's life, the greater the risk that the truth would slip out.

She bit her lip but the facts had to be faced. She could end up losing this precious child if she cared too much about his uncle's feelings.

CHAPTER SIX

JOSH was getting restless so Felipe pulled out the plug and let the water drain away. Reaching for a towel, he swaddled the baby in it and lifted him out of the bath. There was a changing table against one wall so he laid him down on it.

Josh regarded him with big solemn eyes while his uncle carefully dried him. He didn't seem at all alarmed about being looked after by a stranger, but maybe he had grown used to being handled by different people. Maybe Rebecca had entrusted him to the care of other men who had accompanied her home?

Felipe shut off that thought because it felt wrong to think it. She had been both kind and generous in what she'd said to him, and it didn't feel right to repay her by allowing such thoughts into his head. There was a stack of disposable nappies on a nearby shelf so he helped himself to one and placed it on the table. However, it proved to be incredibly difficult to get the baby into it when he kept squirming about.

Bending, he gave the little boy a mock-ferocious stare. 'We can do this the easy way or the hard way, young man, so which is it to be?'

Josh chortled as he grabbed hold of Felipe's nose and tugged it hard. Felipe winced as he gently unfurled the tiny fingers. 'Mmm, I see. You prefer the hard way, do you?'

Gently grasping the baby's ankles in one hand, he cautiously raised Josh's bottom a fraction so that he could slide the nappy under him. It had been a long time since those lessons with Esmeralda but it worked a treat. He smiled victoriously as he lowered the wriggling baby into position.

'See. All it takes is a little co-operation, *pequeño*.'

He quickly folded over the sections of the nappy and stuck

down the tapes to hold it in place. There was a pile of clean
baby clothes on the shelf as well so he selected a pale blue
sleepsuit and set about getting Josh into it.

He couldn't help thinking how organised everything was—
nappies and clean clothes readily to hand, baby wipes and tal-
cum powder placed where they could easily be reached. It surprised him that Rebecca was so methodical because it didn't
jell with the image he had of her. He found himself looking
for some small anomaly, something missing, but as far as he
could tell she had thought of everything. The only slightly odd
thing was that none of the baby things looked really new.

Felipe frowned as he took another look around. He hadn't
noticed it before, but all of a sudden he realised that everything,
from the changing mat the baby was lying on to the sleepsuit
he was wearing, looked as though it had been purchased second-hand. Although everything was spotlessly clean, the signs
of wear and tear were clear to see now that he was looking for
them. The pattern on the mat was faded in places and the sleepsuit had a neat little darn in its heel.

He felt a wave of anger suddenly surface. What the hell was
going on? Why was his nephew wearing second-hand clothes
when Antonio had left all that money?

'Oh, you didn't need to dress him. That was kind of you.'

He spun round when he heard Rebecca's voice. In a fast
sweep his eyes skimmed over her, searching for evidence of
her perfidy. If she hadn't spent the money on Josh, she must
have spent it on herself.

It was the only logical explanation but, try as he may, he
couldn't find anything to back it up. Nothing she was wearing
looked new or expensive, from the worn denim jeans with their
frayed hems to the faded lemon sweatshirt with its baggy neck-
line.

His gaze moved to her feet in the hope that she might be
wearing designer shoes because at least that would help to
solve the puzzle. But her feet were bare, the pale skin so trans-
lucent that he could see her veins showing through it.

His heart gave the oddest little lurch before he made himself remember that he was supposed to be finding some clue as to what she had done with the money, not letting himself get sidetracked by the sight of her small feet. He deliberately let his eyes track back up her body, but not even a second, more thorough viewing solved the problem.

Her skin was bare of make-up so he could rule out costly cosmetics, and her blonde hair was too natural-looking to be the product of frequent visits to an expensive salon. Even her jewellery was nothing more than a schoolgirlish wristwatch with a worn leather strap. Everything about her appearance hinted at someone who was frugal with money, and it didn't make sense.

If Rebecca hadn't spent Antonio's money on the baby or herself, what had she spent it on?

'Want me to take him? He just needs his bottle then I can put him down for the night…'

Becky trailed off as she became aware of the silence. She felt a shiver work its way down her spine when she saw the way Felipe was staring at her. She wet her lips but it was an effort to ask the question when she knew in her heart that she wasn't going to like the answer.

'Is something wrong?'

'You tell me.' He gave her a slow smile, a world removed from the one he'd given her when he had related that story about the doll.

Becky felt her heart shrivel as though he had just stamped on it, but she tried not to let him see how much it had hurt that he could treat her this way again. Maybe it was foolish, but she'd hoped that they might have got past the point where they each needed to keep scoring points off each other.

'It's a little difficult when I don't know what's going on,' she said stiffly.

'Then maybe it would help if I explained the problem I am having understanding this situation.' He looked pointedly around the bathroom. 'Antonio left you a lot of money—'

'Not that again! For heaven's sake, how many more times do I need to tell you that I never asked him to leave it to me?'

She cuddled Josh to her when she felt him stiffen. He'd sensed she was angry and she didn't want to upset him. However, it was hard not to react when Felipe had seen fit to raise the subject of the money again.

'It was Antonio's decision,' she said more quietly. 'It had nothing whatsoever to do with me.'

'I am not disputing that,' he said calmly, matching his tone to hers. 'My problem is understanding what you spent it on. You mentioned expenses when I asked you the last time, so I can only assume you meant things like clothes and equipment for the baby, maybe some things for yourself, *sí*?'

'Um…yes, that's right.'

She edged towards the door, suddenly uneasy about the direction in which the conversation was heading. She needed some time to work out what she should say, only Felipe obviously didn't intend to wait for an answer. He stepped in front of the door, effectively barring her exit.

'So where are all these expensive things that you bought, Rebecca? Do you have them tucked away in a cupboard somewhere? Do you just get them out on special occasions?'

He flicked a dismissive glance at the changing table with its faded mat, the pile of clean baby clothes, her own outfit, and she willed herself not to give in to the panic she could feel building inside her.

'Nothing I can see in here looks expensive. If I'm not mistaken, most of it has been bought second-hand. So tell me what you spent all that money on, Rebecca, because I want to know.'

Becky took a deep breath but her heart was racing. How on earth could she explain without telling him the truth, that it had all gone to Tara?

Tara's demands had started the moment she'd agreed not to have an abortion. As well as the initial payment of fifty thousand pounds and the monthly allowance she had received, there had been credit-card bills to be paid, plus payments on a flashy little sports car that Tara had bought. And, as if all that wasn't enough, she had visited Antonio on a number of occasions and asked him for more money to buy baby clothes and equipment.

Tara had claimed that even though she wasn't going to keep the baby, she felt it was only right that she should get everything ready for its arrival.

Becky had had her suspicions that very little of it would be spent on the child, although she hadn't said anything to Antonio. He had been far too ill to deal with Tara's lies. It had only been after Josh's birth that she'd discovered that Tara hadn't spent a penny on the child. There had been no clothes, no cot, no pram—nothing. Instead, Becky had been forced to withdraw the last of her savings to buy what was needed.

By that time all that had been left in Antonio's bank account had been Tara's final payment, and she hadn't dared dip into that. Antonio had given Becky power of attorney over his finances and affairs once he became too ill to manage them himself. He'd never realised how much money Tara had taken, and Becky had been careful not to tell him. It would have upset him too much to know that there would be nothing left for her and Josh when he died.

She hadn't been able to afford to buy anything new for the baby so she'd bought everything second-hand and had spent hours washing and scrubbing to make sure it was all fit for Antonio's precious son.

Antonio had never noticed that, but Felipe had. Now she had to think up an explanation that would satisfy him, even if it meant that his opinion of her ended up worse than before.

'It's very expensive, living in London,' she said, deliberately blanking out that last thought because it was the one that hurt most of all. 'Rent is extortionate even in an area like this. Don't forget there were many months when I couldn't work.'

'So Antonio supported you? Fine, but I still cannot understand how in the months since Josh was born you managed to spend so much money and yet have so little to show for it.'

'There were other bills to be paid as well as rent,' she protested. 'Gas, electric, food…'

'*Claro que sí!* Of course! But you must have been living a very lavish lifestyle if you spent all those thousands of pounds on food and heating.'

Becky bit her lip. It was obvious that he didn't believe her and who could blame him? The figures simply didn't add up. But the thought of him digging deeper and uncovering the truth was more than she could bear. There wasn't a doubt in her mind that Felipe would find some way to dispense with her if he discovered that she wasn't Josh's real mother.

'I…I had debts,' she whispered, hating the fact that she was going to have to lie to him. How ironic it was that not only had she taken over Tara's role as Josh's mother but she would have to assume the other woman's lifestyle as well.

'Debts?' He frowned, his black brows drawing together as he stared at her. 'Do you mean that you had bought things that you could not pay for?'

'Yes. It's not easy to manage on a nurse's salary and things…well, things got out of hand. There were credit-card bills to pay and loan payments on a car… All sorts of things.'

She swallowed the knot in her throat, wondering if he would believe her. Surely he must realise that she wasn't the kind of person who bought herself luxuries that she couldn't afford?

'I see. That explains it, then,' he said flatly, and she felt her heart ache when she heard the disdain in his voice. He *had* believed her and even though she knew that she should feel relieved, it hurt to know what kind of an opinion he had of her.

Felipe stepped aside without another word and Becky hurried to the kitchen. She took a bottle of baby milk from the fridge and quickly warmed it. Josh was starting to grizzle because he was tired, but he soon settled down when she took him into the bedroom and sat on the low nursing chair to feed him.

She watched his eyelids droop as he greedily drank the milk, one small hand rhythmically patting the bottle. He was content and happy, secure in his little world with people who loved him.

She would do everything it took to keep him safe, but she wished with all her heart that she could have done things differently. If she'd had a choice she wouldn't have lied to Felipe and be sitting here now, feeling so wretched. Instead, she would have told him the truth about Tara and Josh, and Antonio and the money.

She knew what she would have liked to have done, but it was too risky. Felipe might not understand that she had only ever wanted to help.

Felipe could feel his head starting to ache as he waited for Rebecca to come back. He massaged his temples, praying that he wasn't about to have one of his infrequent migraine attacks. The past two days had been a strain and his body was reacting to the pressure he had been under. However, the flashpoint had been Rebecca's confession and how it had made him feel.

He didn't believe her. It was as simple as that. Rebecca had claimed that she'd spent the money Antonio had left her, paying off her debts, but she'd lied. Why had she chosen to make herself look even worse in his eyes rather than tell him the truth? Was it because the truth would be even more unacceptable?

He swore softly, giving vent to his frustration in a rare outburst which would have shocked his colleagues had they witnessed it. He knew that the people he worked with considered him to be a very cold fish and that his reputation was well deserved. Nevertheless, it was hard to keep his emotions in check right then.

His opinion of Rebecca had improved dramatically after the compassionate way she'd spoken to him earlier, but now he didn't know what to think. Why had she lied to him? What dreadful secret was she keeping? Why did it scare him to death to realise that it had to be something really bad?

An aura of colour suddenly started to shimmer at the outer edges of his vision and he groaned when he realised that it was a migraine attack starting. It had been years since he'd had the last one and he couldn't believe his bad luck that it should happen now. He glanced round as Rebecca came back into the room, but it was difficult to focus on her.

'Josh is asleep,' she said quietly, coming into the room and switching on the lamps. She shot him an uncertain look when he put his hand over his eyes to protect them from the light. 'Are you all right?'

'Fine,' he snapped, hating to show any sign of weakness in front of her when he already felt so vulnerable.

His feelings towards Rebecca had shifted and he was no longer sure that he could be totally dispassionate about this situation. He knew that he should focus solely on doing what was right for Josh, but he couldn't ignore Rebecca's feelings. It mattered to him if she was hurt or scared and afraid. If only she would tell him the truth, maybe there was something he could do to help her...

'You don't look it,' she said bluntly, bending to turn off the lamp nearest to him.

'Do not concern yourself about me, Rebecca,' he said brusquely, struggling to deal with that idea. Why did he want to help her when he should be trying to make her tell him the truth?

It was almost a relief when whirling circles of colour started spinning before his eyes and drove the question from his head. The migraine attack was rapidly getting worse and he groaned when he felt his stomach churn in an all-too-familiar prelude to the next stage. He rose awkwardly to his feet, deeply embarrassed about what was happening, although there was nothing he could do. The attack had to run its course before he would feel any better.

'Here. Let me help you.' She put her arm around his waist and helped him to the bathroom, lifting the lid on the lavatory once she'd propped him against the wall.

'Give me a shout if you need me. I'll just be outside,' she said, briskly making her exit and sparing him the indignity of having her watch him throwing up.

Felipe sluiced his face afterwards, feeling a little better despite his embarrassment. He had been fortunate in the past and had always had a few minutes' warning before an attack had struck, but this one had come out of the blue. It didn't make him feel good to know that Rebecca had witnessed it, but there

was nothing more than kindly concern on her face when he
finally left the bathroom.

'How do you feel now? A bit better, I hope?'

She slid her arm around his waist again, ignoring his murmured protest that he could manage. Felipe held himself rigid
as she helped him back to the living-room. She was so petite
that he was afraid of hurting her if he leant too heavily on her,
yet when he tried to set some distance between them she tightened her hold on him.

A shiver ran through him when he felt her fingers gripping
his waist. He hadn't put his jacket back on after bathing Josh
and he could feel the warmth of her hand through the thinness
of his shirt. Her hand was so small, yet her fingers were surprisingly strong as they held onto him, strong and determined,
too. He had the strangest feeling that, no matter what happened,
Rebecca would do everything she could to help him, that nothing and nobody would get in her way once she had made up
her mind.

Was that how she'd felt about Antonio? he wondered. Had
she been determined to do all she could for his brother and had
that determination stretched as far as having his child?

He'd believed her when she'd told him that having Josh had
given Antonio the will to keep fighting his illness. Somehow,
it just seemed to fit. Maybe Rebecca hadn't had the baby for
monetary gain after all, but to help his brother. The thought
made his head spin all over again.

Rebecca helped him to the sofa and got him settled. Drawing
over a footstool, she lifted his feet onto it then quickly turned
off the lamps so that the room was in darkness.

'Just rest there for a few minutes. I'll make you a cup of
herb tea. It's feverfew. I don't know if you've tried it, but it's
marvellous for headaches and migraine attacks.'

'Thank you.' Felipe closed his eyes as she hurried away,
wondering if he was behaving like a fool. There was no proof
that Rebecca had had the baby for Antonio's sake. Everything
he'd learned so far was against it, in fact. Even the concern
she'd shown him that night might have been nothing more than

a means to improve his opinion of her. Yet no matter how he tried to rationalise it, the feeling that he might have misjudged her wouldn't go away.

She came back a few minutes later with a steaming cup of liquid which she placed on the table next to him. 'It's too hot to drink at the moment so let it cool down.'

Felipe didn't open his eyes because it was easier to keep them shut. The darkness always helped when he had a migraine attack and he really didn't want her seeing how confused he felt...

He jumped when he felt something cool touch his forehead. His eyes flew open and a ripple ran through him when he found her bending over him. 'What are you doing?' he demanded, putting up a restraining hand.

She gently moved his hand out of the way. 'I'm going to massage your head. It's a technique we use with the children sometimes. Most headaches, even some migraines, are triggered by tension and it helps the muscles to relax.'

'There is no need,' he said shortly, wondering why the thought of her touching him had caused such a violent reaction. His heart was hammering far too fast and his veins felt as though they might burst as the blood pounded through them.

'I know there isn't. But why suffer if there's a chance that I can help you?'

Her voice was so quiet, so uncontentious that he found it difficult to argue. He closed his eyes again, feeling every nerve in his body tense when he felt her hands moving over his forehead. His nose wrinkled when an unfamiliar scent assailed his nostrils.

'What are you using?'

'A few drops of lavender oil, mixed with some almond oil to act as a carrier for it,' she replied softly, gently stroking his temples.

'And do you believe these oils help?' he asked, although it was difficult to keep his mind on the conversation when her hands were having such a marvellous effect. He was already starting to feel a lot more relaxed and his head wasn't hurting nearly as much as it had been doing.

'Oh, yes. Aromatherapy has been proved to help in many cases. There have been studies done which prove how much benefit people can derive from the use of essential oils.'

Felipe frowned because he couldn't help feeling sceptical about that claim. 'In what way can they help?'

'Well, take my own department—Intensive Care—for instance. There was a French study carried out a few years ago which proved that tea tree oil can have beneficial effects in treating MRSA. Highly resistant bacterial infections like that are a nightmare in any IC unit. They inhabit the artificial ventilators and cause real problems for post-operative patients. Most essential oils are antiseptic, as you probably know, and we use tea tree oil quite a lot at St Leonard's. We've found that it makes a big difference.'

'Really?' Despite himself, Felipe was intrigued.

'Yes, really. You just have to put aside all your preconceived ideas about it being a lot of mumbo-jumbo. People have used the oils from plants for thousands of years to help cure them, so why should modern-day patients be any different?'

'It sounds as though you have studied this,' he said softly, sighing when he felt her fingers gently massaging his skull. The effect was so wonderfully soothing that he almost groaned out loud, but he managed to stop himself at the very last moment.

'I did a course after I left my previous post. I'd been working in an IC unit but it was closed down as part of a cost-cutting exercise. I'd always been interested in the use of oils and herbal medicines so I decided to get a grounding in the basics.'

She moved her fingers across his scalp in a gentle, circular motion. 'I was working for an agency at the time. It was mainly night work so I was able to study during the day.'

Felipe frowned. He couldn't help thinking that it had needed a great deal of dedication to study whilst holding down a job. It jarred to think of Rebecca doing that. It didn't fit in with the image of a woman who'd claimed to have squandered a fortune on luxuries. Suddenly he was more convinced than ever that she'd lied to him about the money, but how could he make her tell him the truth?

'How does that feel now? Any easier?'

He jumped when she spoke, only then realising that she'd finished the massage. He cautiously opened his eyes, but his headache was nowhere near as bad as it had been.

'Much better. Thank you,' he said formally.

'Good.' She came around the sofa and smiled at him. 'Now, drink that tea and you'll feel even better, I guarantee it.'

He picked up the cup, grimacing as he took a tentative sip of the hot liquid. Rebecca laughed softly, a musical sound which for some reason made his stomach muscles clench.

'You look just like Josh does when I try to introduce some new food to his diet. Be brave and drink it all up. I promise that it won't poison you.'

'Even though it would solve a lot of your problems if you managed to get rid of me from your life?' he suggested drily, taking another sip of the tea.

'We can't always have everything we want, can we? We all have to compromise at times.'

He put down the cup and looked at her because there had been something in her voice that told him it hadn't been an idle statement. It was dark in the room with just the light from the skylight to chase away the shadows. Rebecca was wiping the oil from her hands on an old towel and she didn't look at him even though she must have known he was looking at her.

Felipe found himself wishing that he could tell what she was thinking, but her face was little more than a blur, her soft, blonde hair falling around it. Maybe it was the fact that she looked so young and vulnerable at that moment which made him oddly hesitant about demanding an explanation. Or maybe the truth was that he didn't want another confrontation that night. Whatever, his tone was gentler than it might otherwise have been.

'Meaning that I will need to compromise as well as you?'

'Yes.' She shrugged but there was an air of tension about

her all of a sudden which made his skin prickle. 'We shall both have to compromise if this is going to work. You want me to go to Mallorca to live and I've decided that's what I shall do, but there are conditions.'

'What kind of conditions?' he asked flatly, because he refused to let her see how that statement had worried him.

'That I have the final say where Josh is concerned. I know how easy it would be for you to take over, Felipe. You're used to doing things your way, but you have to accept that I know what's best for Josh. I'm happy for you to play a role in his life, but it has to be on my terms.'

He heard Rebecca take a deep breath and he felt his stomach muscles tighten as he waited to hear what else she had to say.

'You have to remember that you're his uncle, not his father. I know what Antonio wanted for Josh and I intend to see that his wishes are respected.'

'And you believe that I would try to override my brother's wishes?' It was impossible to keep the hurt out of his voice and he heard her sigh.

'I don't believe that you would do it intentionally, Felipe. I know how much you loved Antonio and how upset you've been because you believe that you let him down. But trying to compensate by using Josh as a substitute for your brother would be wrong. Josh is Josh. He's a person in his own right.'

He didn't know what to say. Was she right? Had he been hoping to ease his grief over his brother's death by taking control of his nephew's future? He couldn't dispute it but didn't want to agree with it either, and it was his own inability to know how he felt which worried him most. It simply wasn't like him to be so indecisive.

He stood up, knowing that he needed some time on his own to think about everything that had happened that night. Rebecca didn't try to stop him as he left the room. She followed him into the hall and opened the front door.

'I'll speak to you tomorrow to finalise the arrangements,' she said quietly, and he nodded because he didn't trust himself to speak.

She suddenly reached up on tiptoe and he felt shock score through him when she brushed his cheek with her lips. It was the first time that she'd touched him of her own volition and it felt like a turning point, as though from that moment their relationship would be on a different footing. The idea worried him and it must have shown.

'Don't look so worried, Felipe. Everything will work out if we really want it to.'

He heard the plea in her voice but exactly what did she want him to believe? That the situation would work out as she'd said it would? Or that she really *cared* how he felt after everything that had been said between them, all the insults and harsh words?

He left the flat and made his way downstairs. The streetlights were on and he wondered if it was the light from them which had made his vision blur again until he realised it was the tears in his eyes. In his heart he knew that he might be making a mistake but he couldn't help it. He *wanted* to believe that Rebecca cared about his feelings, wanted it so much that it scared him to acknowledge the depth of his need.

What did it mean? Surely he couldn't be falling under her spell the same way Antonio had?

CHAPTER SEVEN

'THERE will need to be an inquest, of course. Highly regrettable, but one can understand the parents' distress. One minute they're told that their daughter should make a full recovery and the next they're being told that she's died because of some dreadful blunder.'

Becky sighed as she looked around the office at all the gloomy faces. Little Rosie Stokes had died during the night, despite all their efforts to redress the damage caused by the wrong blood transfusion. As if that wasn't bad enough, the staff from St Ada's were claiming that she'd been given the wrong transfusion on admission to St Leonard's and that they weren't to blame for what had happened. It meant that everyone involved would need to give a statement.

'Just what we need, I don't think,' Karen declared as they left the office.

Sister Reece was back on duty that day so Becky had left her to deal with an irate James Watts. The consultant was furious that even a hint of blame might be attached to him and his staff, and intended to get to the bottom of the affair. Simon was in the office with them and he rolled his eyes at her as she passed the window.

She gave him a quick smile and hurried into the ward. Simon had been trying to get her on her own all morning but so far she'd managed to avoid him. He obviously wanted to talk about what had happened when she'd introduced him to Felipe but, frankly, she didn't want to discuss it. She had enough problems without adding any more.

A frown pleated her brows as for the hundredth time she found herself wondering why she'd kissed Felipe. At the time it had seemed the most natural thing to do. It was only after

shutting the front door that she'd started wondering what had
prompted her to do such a thing. Had it been simply a way to
comfort him because he'd been upset?

She'd tried to tell herself that all night long, but she knew
in her heart that it hadn't been the only reason. There was
something about Felipe that drew her to him, and it scared her
to have to admit that it wasn't just because he bore a striking
resemblance to Antonio.

'You don't believe what Ada's lot are saying, do you,
Becky?'

Becky looked up, realising that she'd missed what Karen had
said. 'Sorry, what was that?'

'I asked you if you believed what the staff from St Ada's
are saying—about it being our fault, not theirs.' Karen frowned.
'What *is* the matter with you today? You've been miles away.
There's nothing wrong with Josh, is there?'

'No, he's fine. I'm just a bit distracted, I suppose.' She took
a quick breath, realising this was the perfect opportunity to
break the news of her departure. 'I'm handing in my notice
today. I've decided to move to Mallorca at the end of the
month.'

'So it is true? Simon mentioned something about it yesterday
but I thought he was having me on because you hadn't said
anything to me.'

Becky bit back a sigh when she heard the hurt note in
Karen's voice. 'I never had a chance because we were so busy
all day long. I only told Simon because we happened to be
sitting together at lunchtime.'

'Oh, that explains it, then. I was a bit miffed that you'd told
him and not me. Mind you, I did wonder if you'd told him that
to sort of gee him up,' Karen said cheerfully, taking Danny
Epstein's notes from the end of his bed and quickly writing
down his obs.

The boy had come through the operation to replace his damaged heart valves far better than anyone had dared to hope and
was starting to show signs of improvement. His parents had
been so encouraged by his progress, in fact, that they'd taken

a break that morning, having spent the whole week at his bedside.

Becky smiled as she checked the readings as Karen jotted them down. 'He's doing really well, isn't he?'

'He is, but stop trying to change the subject. We were talking about you and Simon.' Karen hung the clipboard back in its place and looked at her. 'So?'

'So what?' She sighed when her friend rolled her eyes in exasperation. 'There is no me and Simon, and I wasn't trying to "gee him up", as you so eloquently put it. We're just friends, that's all.'

'Maybe that's how you feel, but I have the distinct impression that Simon was hoping to be rather more than just a friend,' Karen retorted.

'I don't have time for a relationship,' she said bluntly. 'I have my work cut out trying to hold down a full-time job and take care of Josh.'

'But you'll have a bit more time when you move to Mallorca?' Karen suggested. 'I can see why you've decided it might be a good idea. I expect Josh's uncle will help you look after him so you'll have some time for yourself. Families come in very handy at times, don't they?'

'They do,' Becky murmured, not wanting to be drawn into a discussion about the extent of Felipe's involvement.

Would he accept what she'd said about her being in charge of any decisions concerning Josh's future? she wondered as they moved to the next bed. Or would he try to usurp her authority once she was living in Mallorca?

It was impossible to guess, but it was unsettling to think that she might have a fight on her hands. Becky tried to put it out of her mind while she concentrated on her work, but it was an unsettling day all round.

James Watts got in touch with the consultant at St Ada's and it appeared that the blood that had been given to Rosie hadn't come from them. Each 500 ml unit of blood was bar-coded so it could be traced back to its source, and their records showed that it had come from St Leonard's supplies.

Becky was called into the office to explain what had gone on from the minute the child had been admitted to the IC unit. Although she hadn't dealt with the transfer herself, she had been in overall charge at the time. Karen had been responsible for settling the little girl and she'd had Debbie to help her. When Karen had been called away, the trainee had been left on her own.

Debbie was interviewed, but she categorically denied having changed the transfusion. As she pointed out, Rosie had arrived with a transfusion already set up and there had been no need to fetch a fresh unit of blood when more than half of it had been left. How the child had ended up with blood that had come from St Leonard's was a mystery, but Becky knew that there needed to be an investigation.

It left everyone feeling very edgy so it was a relief when it was time to go home. She had a word with Debbie and tried to reassure her that she wasn't being blamed for what had happened, but it was obvious that the trainee was upset about being under suspicion.

Becky left the hospital at a little after six, half expecting to find Felipe waiting for her. There was no sign of him so she collected Josh and took him home. They went through their usual night-time routine and all the while she kept waiting for the phone to ring. However, by the time she'd settled Josh for the night, Felipe still hadn't contacted her. She was making herself some supper when there was a knock on the door.

Her heart was hammering as she hurried to answer it because she had no idea what she would say if Felipe raised the matter of that kiss. How could she explain if he demanded to know why she'd done it? Telling him that it had felt like the right thing to do sounded a very lame excuse. It was a relief to discover that it wasn't Felipe after all, but a neighbour from the flat downstairs with a package for her.

She went back to the kitchen and opened it, staring in bewilderment at the two plane tickets. There was one for her and one for Josh, first-class seats for a one-way trip to Mallorca at the end of the month. There was an envelope as well and inside it there was a cheque for twenty thousand pounds.

Becky ripped open the package but there was nothing else, not even a note. Felipe had simply sent her everything she needed. A few kindly words of reassurance that she was doing the right thing obviously hadn't featured on his list of essentials. It hurt to realise that he could ignore her feelings when she cared so much about his.

She felt her breath catch as that thought sank in. When had she stopped seeing him as a threat and started worrying about him as a person? Had it been last night when she'd kissed him? She wasn't sure, but she knew in her heart that her feelings towards him had changed in the past three days.

It worried her because she couldn't afford to start having doubts at this stage. She had to think about Josh and making sure that he was safe.

Josh needed her. She had to hold onto that thought and know in her heart that everything she'd done had been justified. And yet she couldn't help wondering how Felipe would feel if he found out the truth, if he would be hurt as well as angry because she had lied to him.

She cared how he felt, she realised. She cared a great deal.

'Dr Valdez! This is a surprise.'

Felipe smiled thinly when he heard the shock in Domingo Santiago's voice. It was obvious that the younger doctor hadn't been expecting him to turn up at the Clinica Valdez at that time of the night. It was a little after eleven and it was rare for him to arrive so late unless there was an emergency. However, he'd felt a deep reluctance to go home after the taxi had brought him back from the airport. He had been too on edge to sit in the villa with only his thoughts for company.

'I thought I would check to see if there have been any problems in my absence, Dr Santiago. Have we had many new admissions while I was away?'

He followed the younger man across the foyer, deliberately cleansing his mind of any thoughts except what might have happened at the clinic in his absence. He had spent hours going over what had happened the night before, recalling time after time how Rebecca had kissed him. Even now he could taste the sweetness of her lips, remember with an alarming clarity just how soft they'd felt. If he'd allowed himself to he could have conjured up her image as well, seen in his mind's eye her beautiful face, her soft grey eyes, the sweetness of her smile...

'Sadly, yes. It has been extremely busy.'

He blinked when he realised that Domingo was speaking. He felt a shudder run through him as he realised how easily his thoughts had returned to Rebecca even though he'd been determined not to think about her. It was an effort to respond with an outward show of calm when his heart was racing.

'Indeed? And has anything serious happened?'

'This morning there was a particularly nasty accident in the bay. A man overturned one of those jet-skis which are so popular with the tourists at the moment.' Domingo sighed. 'He suffered a broken collar-bone and some cuts and bruises, but his son was far more seriously injured. The child has a fractured skull and I needed to operate on him.'

Felipe's mouth thinned. There had been several bad accidents involving jet-skis in the past year.

'People do not seem to understand the risks they take,' he said shortly, pressing the button to summon the lift. 'If one hits water whilst travelling at speed the impact is every bit as great as crashing into a brick wall and can have equally devastating consequences.'

'I know.' Domingo sounded a little nervous as they got into the lift and sent it on its way to the children's department.

Felipe bit back a sigh when he realised that the younger doctor had picked up on his tension and was afraid that he'd done something to upset him. It wasn't true, of course. He was just feeling out of sorts because of everything that had happened of late. Why *had* Rebecca kissed him?

The thought slid into his mind again and he groaned then hurriedly covered it with a cough when he saw Domingo's alarmed expression. 'I would like to take a look at the child if you don't mind, Dr Santiago. Not that I am in any doubt that you have done everything possible to help him.'

'*Claro que sí!* Of course.' Domingo looked pleased as they left the lift and made their way to the child's room.

Felipe smiled to himself because he couldn't help thinking how odd it was that a few words could soothe someone's fears. He knew that the younger man was somewhat in awe of him and resolved to be more aware of that in his dealings with Domingo in future.

It was an idea that would never have crossed his mind a few days earlier and he frowned when he realised it. Was it Rebecca's influence again? he found himself wondering as they made their way into the room where the child lay unconscious. Maybe. It was disturbing to realise the effect she was having on his life.

The boy's parents were sitting with their son so Felipe put aside his own problems while he spoke to them. They were hollow-eyed with grief and he was shocked when he found his own emotions welling to the surface. There was actually a lump in his throat when he saw the mother's distress and tears in his own eyes when the father broke down and cried.

What was happening to him? he wondered. Why did he feel things so acutely all of a sudden? Was this *all* due to Rebecca? Did her influence extend to this area of his life as well?

It was an effort to hide his dismay as he assured the worried parents that everything possible was being done for their child. They looked a little better when he took his leave of them and Domingo remarked on it as they left the room.

'It helped to have a word with you, sir. Silvia and I have done our best to reassure them, but it's a very worrying time for them. At least you have managed to set their minds at rest.'

Felipe nodded, appreciating the fact that the younger man had seen fit to say anything. 'Thank you, Domingo, but if there is any credit due, it must go to you. You did an excellent job on the child. If he recovers—which I am in no doubt that he will—it will be thanks to your skill.'

'*Gracias!*' Domingo sounded stunned. He was obviously

overcome at being complimented twice in one night and looked relieved when his beeper sounded. He hurried off to A and E to deal with a new casualty while Felipe took himself to his office.

He closed the door then looked around the room. Everything was exactly as he'd left it, his desk still neatly stacked with papers, his white coat hanging on the coat-stand, and yet it all looked different, strange, as though the few days he had been away had made him see it through new eyes. This had been his world for so many years yet all of a sudden he found himself wondering if it was all he wanted from life. Surely there should be more than this rather sterile existence?

Unbidden, an image of Rebecca slid into his mind once again and he sighed because it was pointless trying to shut it out. He may as well think about her rather than fight it, remember how she'd looked last night with her feet bare and her blonde hair falling around her face, remember once again how sweetly sensual her lips had felt when they'd brushed his cheek.

A pulse started beating low in his stomach and he shifted uncomfortably, but it didn't ease. It just grew stronger, turned into the throbbing ache which he hadn't felt for so long that it stunned him to feel it then. To feel his body growing hot with desire and know it was for the woman whom he had always believed had used his brother shocked him, but he couldn't stop what was happening any more than he could have stopped breathing.

He wanted Rebecca, wanted her as a man wanted a woman, wanted her in the basest yet the most wonderful of ways, and nothing he could do would stop this hunger growing inside him.

Felipe took a deep breath, let it out slowly, did it all over again a dozen more times, and after a while the feeling began to recede. Moving around the desk, he sat in the big leather chair and thought about what had happened and what it might mean.

Maybe he was sexually frustrated because it had been a while since he had slept with a woman, but he couldn't in all honesty claim that as the explanation. He had encountered other beautiful women in the past but they hadn't stirred him the way Rebecca did.

That was the reason why he'd not gone to see her before he'd left London. He'd been afraid that she would guess how mixed up he felt about that kiss, afraid that she might use it to her advantage and his detriment. He might respond to Rebecca on many levels but he didn't trust her, not yet, not until he'd found out why she had lied to him about the money. And it was the fear of what he might uncover that now caused him such anguish.

He didn't want to find a reason to hate her.

The phone suddenly rang and he quickly reached for the receiver. He listened intently while Domingo outlined the new casualty's injuries then brusquely interrupted him. 'I shall be straight there. Get the patient ready for Theatre.'

He stood up and if he felt a sense of relief at being spared any more soul-searching he made no apologies for it. He would be able to deal with Rebecca and the effect she had on him so much better if he got himself back on track.

Josh had grizzled steadily throughout the flight. He was normally such a good baby that it was a surprise how fretful he had been that day. Becky had done her best but nothing had seemed to soothe him.

Maybe he'd picked up on her own mood, she thought as the plane began its descent into Palma airport. She had been on edge for the past three weeks, waiting for this day to come, dreading its arrival. Considering this was the first step on the way to a new life for them both, she couldn't claim that she felt happy about it.

The plane finally landed and by that time Josh was screaming in earnest. Becky smiled her thanks when the man in the next seat helpfully carried her flight bag while she struggled to hang onto Josh.

She made her way to the baggage reclaim area while Josh roared his disapproval. Fortunately, another person lifted her case off the carousel and put it on a trolley for her. She pushed it through customs, hoping there would be someone at the airport to meet her.

She had sent a fax to the clinic, confirming that she would be on the flight, so hopefully Felipe would have arranged for a taxi to collect her. However, it wasn't until she spotted him standing on the fringes of the crowd that she realised he'd decided to come himself.

Becky felt her heart give the most peculiar jolt as she watched him striding towards her. He was wearing a light grey suit that day and he stood out from the crowd of casually dressed holidaymakers. She saw two young women turn and look at him as he passed, but he ignored them as he made his way straight to her.

'Is there something wrong with Josh? I could hear him screaming while you were collecting your luggage.'

'He's probably upset because of the change to his routine,' she replied, trying not to let him see how aware of him she was. It was three weeks since she had seen him and now she was struck by how tall he was, how imposing, how very handsome. It was hard not to stare at him but not for the life of her would she let him guess what was going through her mind.

'Are you sure he isn't sick?' he asked worriedly, laying a gentle hand on Josh's forehead. 'He feels very hot.'

'That's because he's got himself into a real tizz,' she replied, shifting the baby onto her other hip. He was getting heavy now and it was quite tiring, having to carry him.

'A tizz?' Felipe repeated uncertainly.

'Grumpy, angry, fretful, all sort of mixed up together,' she explained, then looked at him in surprise when he laughed.

'Ah, I understand exactly how he feels, *pobrecito*.'

Becky frowned because she wasn't sure what he'd meant by that. She looked at him questioningly and was surprised when she saw a little colour darken his cheeks before he briskly took charge of the trolley.

'This way. I managed to park near the entrance so it isn't far to walk.'

She followed him in silence, wondering why her heart seemed to be playing hopscotch across her ribs all of a sudden. Had that been a reference to the fact that Felipe himself had been feeling grumpy and mixed up, perhaps?

She sensed it was so and also guessed that the reason for his mood owed itself to something she had done. Had it been that kiss? Had it caused him as many sleepless nights as it had caused her? Frankly, she couldn't believe how one chaste kiss could have caused such havoc, for him as well as her.

The sun was brilliant when they stepped outside. Josh let out a shriek as the bright light assailed his eyes and Becky hastily shook off the moment of introspection. He buried his face in her shoulder, screaming harder than ever when she tried to console him.

Felipe shot the baby a worried look as he unlocked the car. 'Does he want a drink, perhaps, or something to eat?'

'Probably both. He wouldn't have anything on the plane, but maybe he'll have some juice now. It's worth a try.'

She tried to retrieve the bottle of fruit juice from her shoulder-bag, but it was hard to unzip it with the baby clinging to her. Felipe quickly stepped forward and took Josh from her, jiggling him up and down in his arms while she found the bottle.

Becky smiled when she heard him talking to the child, telling him that he would soon be home and that there was no need to cry. It was doubtful if Josh was listening to a word he said as he roared his displeasure, but that didn't seem to deter Felipe from trying. Frankly, she was touched by his obvious concern for the little boy. There would be few men who would willingly try to calm a screaming infant the way he was doing.

'Get into the car and I'll pass him to you,' he instructed when she had found the bottle. 'I've had a baby-seat fitted into the back and he will be safer in that than on your knee.'

'Thanks,' she replied, grateful for his thoughtfulness.

She took Josh from him and quickly strapped him into the comfy little seat. Taking the top off the bottle, she let a few drops of the juice dribble onto the baby's lips. He stopped crying immediately and reached for the bottle.

She let him hold it, keeping a careful watch on him while Felipe got into the car and started the engine. He turned on the air-conditioning so that within minutes the interior of the car felt blissfully cool. She sighed in relief.

'That's better! Even Josh is starting to feel a bit better now, aren't you, sweetheart?'

She buzzed the baby's downy cheek with a kiss then looked up and found that Felipe was watching her in the rear-view mirror. She felt herself blush because she couldn't help thinking about the way she'd kissed *his* cheek. What made it worse was that she knew he was remembering it as well.

It was a relief when he looked away and busied himself with pulling out of the parking space. They left the airport and he turned onto a busy main road. It was midday and a lot of holiday flights had landed. The road was crowded with taxis and coaches ferrying people to their hotels and apartments.

Becky stared out of the window, thinking about the last time she'd travelled this route on her way back from the Clinica Valdez after that first unhappy meeting with Felipe. She had never imagined that she would be making a return trip, certainly hadn't expected to be living on the island a few weeks later. Had she done the right thing by coming here?

Just for a moment she was assailed by panic before she forced herself to calm down and consider the facts. She would never have got hold of the money to pay Tara if she hadn't agreed to come to Mallorca. She had deposited a cheque for twenty thousand pounds in the woman's bank account, and as far as she was concerned that was the end of the matter, although she doubted if Tara saw it that way.

Tara would, no doubt, make more demands at some point, but now she wouldn't know where to find her and Josh. Becky had taken care not to leave a forwarding address at the flat and had told nobody, apart from the people she worked with, where she was going. Of course, there was always a chance that Tara would go to the hospital and ask for her new address, but she

would deal with that problem if it arose. For a few months, at
least, Josh would be safe.

'He seems to have settled down now.'

She looked up when Felipe spoke, once again feeling her
heart surge when she saw him watching her in the mirror.
'Um…yes. He's worn out, poor little scrap.'

'It will take a few days for him to adjust to his new sur-
roundings,' he said levelly, returning his attention to the road.
'He is bound to be a little fractious at first.'

'Probably. I suppose I've been spoilt really,' she said, gently
easing the bottle out of Josh's hand. His eyelids were drooping
and it was obvious that he was about to doze.

'Why do you say that?' Felipe asked, his deep voice filled
with curiosity.

'Because Josh has been such a good baby right from the
start. He rarely cried even when he was just a few days old,
and especially not when Antonio was looking after him.'

She smiled as she brushed a wispy curl off the baby's flushed
little cheek. 'I think he sensed that his daddy was ill and he
wanted to help him.'

'Do you think a child is capable of sensing things like that?'
he asked, and she frowned when she heard how gruff his voice
had sounded. Did he think she was crazy to suggest such a
thing? she wondered, shooting him a wary glance.

It came as a surprise when she realised that there wasn't a
trace of scepticism on his face. It was only when his eyes met
hers in the mirror that she could see the emotion they held and
realised that he'd been deeply moved by the idea.

'Yes, I do. Babies are very receptive to mood. Everyone
knows that they react to anger and laughter so why shouldn't
they respond to other emotions? It's only as we grow older that
we develop a need to hide our feelings.'

'Maybe we come to realise that it can be dangerous to show
how we feel, Rebecca. There are always people who are ready
to take advantage of our weakness.'

'I don't think it's a sign of weakness to show one's feelings,'
she protested.

She frowned because she sensed that the comment had been a personal one rather than a general statement. Had something happened to Felipe in the past that had taught him not to show his emotions?

It might be the key to understanding Felipe better if she found out the answer. Without stopping to think about what she was doing, she leant forward in the seat.

'Did somebody take advantage of you, Felipe? Is that why you try to distance yourself from people?'

CHAPTER EIGHT

FELIPE felt a nerve start to tick in his jaw. He knew that Rebecca was waiting for him to answer, but for the life of him he didn't know what to say.

He had never spoken about his hurt when he'd found out how Teresa had deceived him all those years ago and would have denied that it had influenced his behaviour in the intervening years. But suddenly he could see the effect it had had on him.

Discovering that his fiancée had been having an affair with his best friend had been a shock, even though he'd realised eventually that he had been partly to blame. He had been so busy with his work and looking after Antonio that Teresa had grown tired of being ignored and had sought consolation elsewhere.

He had learned a valuable lesson from the experience, though, and had made up his mind never again to mix love with the demands of his job. The breakdown of his relationship with Teresa had affected everything he did. It was the reason why he needed to be in control all the time and the motivation for choosing the kind of life he led. If he hadn't let it affect him, surely he would have had more in his life by now than just his work at the clinic?

'I'm sorry. I really shouldn't have asked you a question like that. I didn't mean to be rude.'

He heard the apology in her voice but it didn't disguise the concern he could hear in it as well. The nerve in his jaw beat all the harder. Rebecca cared—really *cared*—about what had happened to him, and it touched his heart to realise it.

It was on the tip of his tongue to pour out the whole story when a taxi suddenly cut in front of him, causing him to swerve

106

sharply to avoid a collision. He heard Rebecca gasp with fright and little Josh give a great wail as he was jolted awake.

Drawing in to the side of the road, he turned to look at them both, and felt his heart swell with tenderness when he saw how Rebecca was fussing over the baby and ignoring the fright she'd had. She was such a good mother, kind and loving, always putting the child's welfare before her own. The thought shocked him to the core so that it was an effort to respond when she looked up.

'He's OK. He just had a bit of fright, didn't you, poppet?' She kissed the baby's chubby little fist then blew a raspberry on his palm, smiling when Josh gave a reluctant chuckle. Lifting the hem of his blue T-shirt, she blew another raspberry on the child's tummy and laughed when Josh gurgled with delight.

'See, you're fine now, aren't you, darling? And it won't be long before your Uncle Felipe shows you his beautiful clinic. Won't that be fun?'

Felipe found himself smiling as he listened to her. Josh couldn't possibly understand what she was saying, but the child responded to the tone of her voice. She *was* a good mother and there was no denying that, even though it caused him some anguish to admit it.

If Rebecca was such a good mother and such a caring person, why had she felt it necessary to lie to him about the money? What was she trying to cover up?

The thought had plagued him for the past three weeks but all of a sudden he knew that he had to find out the answer. If there was anything he could do to help her, he would.

His heart jolted as he started the car, but there was no way that he could lie to himself. He wanted to help Rebecca because he cared about her. If someone had told him a few short weeks ago that he would be in this situation, he would have laughed. However, he didn't feel like laughing now. Finding out the truth about Rebecca was even more important now than it had been in the beginning.

It didn't take them very long to reach the clinic after that. Felipe drove straight to his house and drew up outside. He got out and helped Rebecca from the car, automatically taking Josh from her.

'Is this where you live?' she asked, taking a long look around.

She raised her hand to shade her eyes as she stared across the bay, and he felt his stomach clench when he saw how the action had made her small breasts press against the soft cotton of her white T-shirt. She wasn't wearing a bra and he could see the outline of her nipples through the thin fabric. His mouth suddenly went dry so that it was an effort to act as though nothing was wrong when she turned to him.

'It's absolutely beautiful, Felipe! The view is superb. Are Josh and I staying near here? I do hope so because it would be marvellous to wake up each morning to a view like that.'

'Then you will be pleased to hear that you and Josh will be living right here in the villa.'

He summoned a smile but it alarmed him to know how quickly he'd responded to her. He could have had his pick of women over the years but, apart from a few brief liaisons, he'd preferred not to complicate his life. Yet he only had to look at Rebecca and his blood started racing, his heart started pounding and his head began to fill with all kinds of crazy ideas.

'Come, I shall show you to your rooms.'

He slid his hand under her elbow to lead her towards the house, praying that she couldn't tell that he was in such turmoil. He had to find a way to stop himself thinking about her all the time, but it wasn't going to be easy. All of a sudden he found himself wondering if he'd made a mistake by bringing her to Mallorca.

How long would he be able to keep his distance from her when she would be living in his house?

Becky felt her heart give one great bounding leap as Felipe put his hand under her elbow. She quickly jerked away and stared at him in dismay.

'What do you mean—Josh and I will be living here? You made no mention of that when I agreed to come here.'

'We never discussed where you would be living, as I recall,' he said calmly, although she could see the impatience in his sherry-brown eyes. It was obvious that he wasn't pleased that she'd seen fit to question his arrangements, but hard luck. Living with Felipe definitely hadn't been part of their bargain.

She opened her mouth to tell him in no uncertain terms that she wouldn't be staying at the villa when an elderly woman suddenly appeared. She rushed down the steps towards them, exclaiming in rapid Spanish when she saw Josh. Holding out her arms, she took the baby from Felipe and hugged him to her.

Josh responded with one of his most angelic smiles as the woman carried him indoors. Becky had no option but to follow and found herself in a huge black-and-white tiled hall. Although the villa was obviously new, the decor was traditional and very Spanish, with lots of dark carved woodwork offset by starkly white walls on which several beautiful watercolours in ornate gilt frames were hung.

She automatically stopped to look around then realised that she was in danger of getting sidetracked. She turned to Felipe, who had followed with her luggage. 'You should have told me that you expected us to stay with you.'

'I realise that and I apologise. It simply never occurred to me that it would create a problem.'

He smiled at the elderly woman, who had hesitantly come forward to be introduced. 'This is my housekeeper, Maria. As you can see, she adores babies. She was my parents' housekeeper for many years and she loved Antonio. She looked after him when he was a child.'

Becky summoned a smile as she shook the woman's hand, not wanting her to think that she was annoyed with her. It was Felipe she was angry with for not having explained the situation.

'I'm delighted to meet you, Maria,' she said in her careful Spanish. The woman said something to her but she spoke so fast that Becky couldn't catch what she'd said.

'She said that she will be delighted to help you take care of Antonio's son if you will let her,' Felipe explained.

'*Gracias*, Maria,' she replied, feeling a little dizzy from the speed with which everything seemed to be happening.

When Maria suggested taking Josh into the kitchen to find him something to eat, she found herself agreeing because it was easier than arguing. Obviously, this would need sorting out because she couldn't stay at the villa, but right at that moment she didn't have the strength for a full-blown argument.

'I can tell that you are upset, Rebecca, and that was never my intention.'

She turned when he spoke, feeling a shiver run down her spine when she saw the regret in his eyes. It made her feel very strange to realise that he cared about her feelings so it was an effort to focus when he continued.

'I hope that you will bear with me until I can make other arrangements for you and Josh. However, at this time of the year, when the holiday season is under way, it can be difficult to find suitable accommodation, you understand.'

'So long as it doesn't take too long,' she said quickly, not wanting there to be any misunderstanding. Maybe he hadn't meant to upset her, but it would be far too difficult to live in the villa with him for any length of time.

Her heart gave a small hiccup at the thought of them sharing the intimacies that came with living under the same roof, and she hurried on. It wouldn't help to dwell on how it would feel to wake each morning and see Felipe over the breakfast table, to go to bed each night and know that he was sleeping close by. Thoughts like that only confused her.

'I would prefer it if we had a place of our own. And I'm sure that you must enjoy your privacy as much as I do.'

His face closed up and she frowned when she heard the biting note in his voice. 'Rest assured that you are free to do whatever you wish while you are living here. I have no intention of curtailing your social life because you are living under my roof.'

'That wasn't what I meant!' she exploded, her face flaming as she realised what he was suggesting. 'Let's get this straight, Felipe. I am not looking for a social life, as you put it so delicately. My only interest is in making sure that Josh is safe and happy.'

'Then there should be no problem about you staying here

for a short while. Josh's welfare is my only concern, too,' he said smoothly.

Picking up her case, he led the way across the hall and down a wide passageway. Becky followed him because there wasn't much else she could do. He stopped and opened a door, moving aside so that she could enter the room.

'I thought this room would be the most suitable. There is a small dressing room leading off it which I've had converted into a nursery. You will be close at hand if Josh should need you during the night.'

'It's beautiful,' she said simply, looking around.

Once again the style was very Spanish in character, with dark oak furniture, white walls and a tiled floor. The bed was enormous, with an intricately carved headboard and covered with a finely woven spread in shades of cream and gold. There were shutters over the window, which had been closed to keep out the sun, and she gasped in delight when she opened them and saw that she had a stunning view over the bay.

Turning, she hurried across the room and peeked inside the *en suite* bathroom, admiring its buttery-coloured marble walls and floor, then checked out Josh's room, shaking her head in amazement when she saw the cot and the toys, the shelves stacked high with baby things.

'You've thought of everything. I don't know what to say, really I don't.'

She opened one of the cupboards, feeling herself choke up when she saw the rows of beautiful little garments for Josh to wear. How many times had she wished that she could afford to buy him things like these?

'I'm pleased that you are satisfied,' he said calmly, and she laughed shakily.

'I'm amazed! I never expected any of this.'

She glanced round and felt her heart lurch when she saw the way he was watching her with such tenderness in his eyes. It stunned her to have him look at her that way, and it was a relief when Maria appeared, carrying a sleepy-looking Josh.

Becky took the baby from the housekeeper and looked at Felipe. 'I'll put him down for a nap, if you don't mind.'

'Of course.' He glanced at his watch and frowned. 'I need to return to the clinic. Perhaps you would join me there once Josh is asleep? Maria will be happy to look after him so it will be the perfect opportunity to acquaint you with the layout of the building before you start work.'

Was that a reminder that she was expected to earn her keep while she was there? Felipe might have been happy to fill the nursery with luxuries for Josh but she couldn't expect such treatment for herself. The only reason she was there was because of Josh and if Felipe found a good enough reason to get rid of her, he wouldn't hesitate to do so.

Becky felt fear rise sharply inside her so that it was an effort to appear calm. 'Of course. I'll be there as soon as I can.'

'Gracias.' He inclined his head but she saw a faint puzzlement in his eyes, as though he had picked up on her fear and was wondering what had caused it.

She drove that thought from her head because it was pointless worrying about it. Her main concern had to be to make sure that Felipe never found out that she wasn't Josh's real mother. The thought of his anger was scary enough, but it was the thought that his opinion of her would plummet even further which hurt the most.

She didn't want Felipe to think too badly of her, even though she refused to go into the reasons why. Something told her that her life might become even more difficult if she found out the answer.

'This next patient was admitted yesterday. He dived into the shallow end of the swimming pool and broke his neck. There is extensive swelling in the area so the X-rays aren't very clear. However, we are hopeful that the spinal cord hasn't been damaged.'

Felipe led the way into the room, smiling calmly at the young man lying in the bed. There was a metal fame supporting his head and neck and a specially adapted mattress to hold his body still and stop him turning.

'Good afternoon, Mr Jeffries. How are you feeling today?'

'About how you'd expect to feel with a broken neck,' the young man replied laconically.

Felipe heard Rebecca laugh and tensed when she moved nearer to the bed. He was far too aware of her and unable to do anything about it. Now he found his hands clenching when he saw her smile at the young man.

'Bit of a silly thing to do, wasn't it?' she teased. 'It might have been better to check how much water was in there first.'

'Now she tells me!' Richard rolled his eyes. He was a good-looking young man in his twenties, one of a party of ten friends who had come on holiday to the island from Scotland.

Felipe had been impressed by his positive attitude. However, he was less impressed when he saw the appreciation in the young man's eyes as he looked at Rebecca. It was obvious that Richard found her attractive and for some reason he bitterly resented it.

'Why weren't you there when I needed you? I wouldn't have been diving into any rotten old swimming pool if I'd had you to keep me company!'

'Are you sure you didn't kiss the Blarney stone instead of the bottom of the pool?' Rebecca retorted, chuckling.

'I'm gutted,' Richard replied. 'You don't really believe that was a line, do you?'

'I most certainly do. And on a score of one to ten I'd rate it as a five, so my advice is to keep practising.'

Felipe shifted abruptly, trying to curb his growing impatience. The pair were carrying on as though he were invisible, and he didn't appreciate being ignored. Rebecca shot him a questioning look then turned when Richard spoke. Felipe saw her face fill with compassion when she heard the fear that underpinned the young man's voice.

'I might not need to practise if I've damaged my spinal cord. I'm not going to have much pulling power if I end up flat on my back in a hospital bed for the rest of my days.'

'You mustn't think like that,' she said quickly, squeezing his hand. 'Dr Valdez has just told me that he's hopeful that it's only bruising which is causing you not to be able to move your limbs.'

'I didn't know if that was just a way to keep me quiet,' Richard confessed, his eyes welling with tears.

'I told you the truth, Mr Jeffries. The X-rays aren't clear because of the swelling in the affected area, but I am as confident as I can be in the circumstances that your spinal cord hasn't been severed.'

Felipe smiled reassuringly at the young man, wondering how he had let himself be hoodwinked into believing that Richard was coping so well with his accident. If Rebecca hadn't drawn him out, the poor soul might have lain there, worrying himself to death.

It was an unsettling thought and he resolved never to let it happen again as they left the room. He would be more sensitive in future, look past the façade people put up and try to gain a better understanding of how they were feeling.

He sighed because it would never have occurred to him to do that a few weeks ago. It seemed to highlight all the changes that had happened to him of late. He didn't need to search too hard to understand who had brought them about. Having Rebecca in his life had changed everything.

'Where to now?'

He jumped when she spoke, and felt himself tense when her arm brushed his. He could feel the silky blonde hairs on her arm tickling his skin and he swallowed as a surge of awareness rushed through his system.

They had reached the end of the corridor and there was just a set of glass doors ahead leading to the theatres. Domingo and Silvia had a list of routine operations that day. He hadn't been needed because they were perfectly capable of managing without him. However, he suddenly found himself wishing that he could immerse himself in some sort of complex surgery which wouldn't allow him to think about anything else. He knew where he was when it involved his work. It was only in other areas of his life that he seemed to have difficulty coping at the moment.

'Felipe?'

He fixed a smile to his mouth when she prompted him, wishing that he felt anywhere near as calm inside where it mattered.

'The children's department is next. That is where you will be working.'

He led the way through the doors and down the stairs to the floor below, struggling to get himself in check. Life was going to be extremely difficult if he couldn't learn to deal with these feelings Rebecca aroused inside him.

'Do you have an IC unit here?' she asked as they made their way down. They reached the landing and he heard her gasp as her feet skidded on the marble floor when she hurried to keep up with him.

Instinctively, he reached out to steady her, feeling the surge of heat that ran through his palm when his hand closed around her arm. Her skin felt so soft and smooth, he thought wonderingly. He could feel those tiny, golden hairs clinging to his fingers now and had the craziest urge to run his hand over them...

'Oops! That was clumsy of me. I should have worn sensible shoes instead of these sandals.'

He heard the breathy note in her voice and only then realised that he still had hold of her. He let her go abruptly and carried on walking, praying that Rebecca hadn't noticed anything amiss. The thought that she might have guessed how sexually aware he was of her was more than he could bear.

He tried reminding himself who she was as they made their way along the corridor, but it no longer worked because he no longer believed it. He couldn't look at Rebecca and see her as a grasping, mercenary gold-digger any more. His feelings about her were far more complex than that. But even if his mind was having difficulty working out how he felt about her, his body had no such compunctions!

Becky took a deep breath as she followed Felipe into the room. She wasn't sure what had happened, but she was aware of the tension that emanated from him.

She rubbed her arm to ease the odd tingling sensation on her skin, but it refused to go away. She could feel it spreading up her arm until it felt as though every inch of her was tingling. And all because Felipe had touched her? It didn't make sense.

'There's still no change, Dr Valdez. Do you think he'll ever wake up?'

She blinked and it felt as though she were awakening from a trance as the room and its occupants suddenly rushed into focus. Becky felt her heart ache when she saw the worried faces of the two people sitting beside the bed. Their expressions were ones she'd seen far too many times over the years. Fear, guilt, grief—the usual reaction of parents faced with a child's illness.

'Unfortunately, there is no way of knowing when Ryan will recover consciousness,' Felipe was saying quietly. He turned to draw her forward and introduce her.

'This is Staff Nurse Williams. She will be looking after your son in the coming weeks. Miss Williams worked in the paediatric intensive care unit at St Leonard's Hospital in London before she decided to join us at the clinic. We are delighted to have her. She has a great deal of experience in dealing with very sick children.'

Becky hid her surprise at the wonderful build-up. Maybe Felipe had wanted to impress upon the parents that their son was receiving the best possible care, but she had to admit that it was good to have her skills recognised.

'Please, call me Rebecca,' she said, shaking hands with Diane and Tim Palmer. She waved Tim back to his chair when he stood up, pulling up another chair so that she could sit with them. She had found that it helped enormously to be on the same level when talking to people.

'What happened to Ryan?' she asked gently. She knew that she could get all the details from the child's notes, but she also knew that the parents often found it cathartic to talk through what had gone on. It also helped them come to terms with what had happened. Most parents found it difficult to accept when their child was gravely ill and often entered a period of denial. It was better if they could face the facts.

She nodded as Tim Palmer explained how his son had been thrown from the jet-ski and had fractured his skull. Tears streamed down his face while he was telling her the story, but it was better than him bottling up his grief.

Becky turned to Diane while Tim composed himself. 'Has there been any sign that Tim knows you're here?'

'None. I've tried talking to him, tried playing him his favourite music, even telling him about his favourite football team, but he doesn't respond.' Diane wiped her own eyes with a tissue as she looked at her six-year-old son. 'It's as though he's not in his body any longer.'

Becky sighed, wondering if she might be stepping on anyone's toes if she gave her opinion. She glanced at Felipe for guidance but he was standing with his arms folded and a completely neutral expression on his face. She took a deep breath. In for a penny, in for a pound!

'In my experience of dealing with children who are in comas, it's best not to try to stimulate them too soon. The brain needs time to recover from the shock of the accident, a bit like a cut needs time to scab over before it will heal,' she explained gently. 'Don't bombard Ryan with too many different experiences. Just understand that it's going to take time and go slowly.'

'And you think that will help him?' Diane asked uncertainly. 'I mean, you read all these articles in the newspapers about people suddenly recovering from a coma because they've been played a favourite bit of music or something.'

'And things like that do happen.' Becky squeezed the woman's hands. 'Don't give up hope that it will happen in Ryan's case, but give him time. Sit here and hold his hand. Maybe you can talk to him for a little while, but don't overstimulate his brain while it's going through this healing process.'

'What do you think, Dr Valdez?' Tim asked doubtfully. 'Is Rebecca right?'

Becky held her breath because she knew that some doctors didn't agree with the theory even though it had been proved to have positive effects. Would Felipe take the opposite view to the one she had expounded?

'I think there is a lot of truth in what Rebecca said. Many neurologists believe that the brain needs to go through a healing period and now opt for a treatment designed not to overstimulate the patient.' He shrugged. 'Of course, there are still many specialists who prefer the older methods and can produce evidence to back them up.'

Becky let out a sigh of relief that he hadn't seen fit to contradict her. Maybe it was silly, but she would have felt dreadful if he had. If Felipe didn't value her as a person, at least he could value her as a nurse.

It was an effort to hide how much that thought had hurt as Diane and Tim eagerly agreed to try the new system. They left them discussing it and carried on with their tour of the clinic, but Becky couldn't shake off the heaviness that had settled in her heart.

She wanted Felipe to see her as the person she really was, but there was no chance of that happening unless she told him the truth. Even then it might not improve his opinion of her to learn that they had paid Tara for Josh. He might think that Josh should have stayed with Tara and that with a bit of encouragement and support the woman would have come to love him in time.

She had no doubt that would never have happened, but would Felipe believe her if she told him everything Tara had done? It seemed inconceivable that anyone would behave so callously so she could understand if he had difficulty accepting it. After all, she had lied to him once so he might think that she was lying to him again. And she was afraid of what might happen if he didn't believe her.

She could end up losing Josh if Felipe didn't think that she was fit to look after him.

CHAPTER NINE

A WEEK passed and Felipe was pleased to see how easily Rebecca had fitted in at the clinic. She was calm and competent, never getting stressed or upset despite the amount of pressure she was under.

It was one of the busiest periods he could remember since the clinic had opened, and many of the patients they admitted were children. However, she coped with it all in the same professional manner that he couldn't help but admire. It was yet another facet of her character, another query to add to the growing list—could she be the woman he had once believed her to be and still hold down an exacting job like this?

He found himself thinking about that question far too many times throughout the day and it worried him that it should be on his mind so much. However, it was at night when he found the situation most difficult to deal with. Although Rebecca was never intrusive, he couldn't ignore her presence in the villa.

He would hear her talking to Maria when he got home from work, hear her singing to Josh while she bathed him, simply *feel* that she was there. His home no longer felt as though it truly belonged to him because he was so aware of her and, frankly, it was a strain.

He resolved to find her alternative accommodation as soon as possible but, as he'd predicted, there wasn't anything available. It appeared that he would have to wait until the main holiday period was over, and the thought of having her around for all those weeks wasn't a comforting one.

He arrived home very late one evening because they'd had an emergency admission as he'd been about to leave. The patient, an elderly man in his seventies, had had a heart attack

119

on the flight to Palma. He'd been rushed straight to the clinic but, despite all their efforts, had died a short time later.

It had been a distressing incident for everyone involved, and he sighed as he let himself into the villa. What he needed most at that moment was a drink and a couple of hours on his own, but there was dinner to get through first—a dinner with Rebecca while he carefully masked his feelings in case she realised how mixed up he felt. When he heard her footsteps crossing the hall he steeled himself before he turned then felt his heart sink when he saw the grave expression on her face.

'What's happened?' he demanded, hurrying towards her. 'Is it Josh?'

'No, Josh is fine.' She gave him a rather abstracted smile then turned when Maria appeared. It was obvious that the housekeeper had been crying and Felipe watched as Rebecca put her arm around her. She looked up and he saw the worry in her soft grey eyes.

'Maria's son has had an accident. I've phoned for a taxi to take her to the airport but I'd like to go with her if you don't mind. She's never flown before and she's a bit scared by the thought of going on a plane.'

'*Claro que sí!*' He frowned, dredging his mind to recall something about Maria's son. He had an idea that José had moved to mainland Spain to work, but he might be mistaken.

He glanced at Rebecca as the housekeeper hurried away to fetch her overnight case. 'Is José still living on the mainland?'

'Yes. He was due to come home a couple of weeks ago, but he stayed on to help finish the new hotel he's been working on,' she explained. 'He works on construction sites at the big Spanish resorts during the winter then comes back to Mallorca for the summer season and works as a waiter at one of the hotels in Alcudia. Maria has been so looking forward to him coming home and now this has to happen.'

Felipe shook his head, wondering how she'd found out so much in such a short time. Maria had been his housekeeper for years yet he'd had no idea that was how her son earned his

living. It made him feel rather uncomfortable to realise how
little interest he had taken in the past.

'Is everything arranged?' he asked abruptly, hating the fact
that he felt at a disadvantage. 'What about the plane ticket? I
shall pay for it, of course.'

'No, it's all sorted out,' she said quickly as Maria came back.
She linked her arm through the housekeeper's and helped her
to the door as the taxi arrived and beeped its horn. 'Josh has
had his bath and I've put him down for the night, but he seems
a bit restless. If you could keep an eye on him until I get
back…'

'Of course,' he said quickly, following them to the door. He
patted Maria's shoulder, seeing how she clung to Rebecca. It
was obvious they had formed a close bond and he could barely
hide his surprise. Maria was normally very reserved with
strangers, but not with Rebecca, it seemed.

Felipe waved the two women off then went back indoors,
still thinking about it. It was yet another indication that he'd
misjudged Rebecca in the beginning. She was kind and caring,
and the proof of that was the way she had helped Maria that
night. How many people would have done what she had, gone
out of their way to make the arrangements for the flight then
insisted on going to the airport with the old lady?

It made him even more impatient to get to the bottom of
what was going on, but until Rebecca opened up to him there
was little he could do. If he could make her trust him then she
might, finally, tell him the truth. If she did that, they could
move on…

He sighed because he knew how dangerous it was to indulge
in thoughts like that. Letting himself dream that he and
Rebecca might one day have more than just Josh in common
was inviting trouble.

He tried to put it from his mind as he made his way to the
nursery, stopping off *en route* to shed his jacket and tie as he
passed his bedroom. Josh was singing to himself when he went
to check on him, burbling away in baby-talk.

Felipe crept into the nursery but the moment the child saw

him he held up his arms to be picked up. He lifted him out of the cot, tossing him gently into the air and smiling when he heard the baby chortling with delight. He didn't look the least bit sleepy so Felipe took him to the kitchen while he found himself something to eat.

He balanced Josh on his knees while he wolfed down a piece of cold chicken, laughing when the child opened his mouth, obviously hoping for a taste. 'I don't think your mama would want you to have any of this, *pequeño*. Let's see if we can find you something else.'

Lifting Josh onto his shoulder, he investigated the contents of the refrigerator and found a punnet of strawberries in the cooler. He took out a handful, grinning when Josh made a grab for them.

'Ah, so you like these, do you? Come along, then, let's go into the sitting-room and relax while you have your snack.' He placed a plump red berry into the baby's hand and smiled at him again. 'But don't tell your mama or she might tell me off for spoiling you.'

He carried the baby into the sitting-room and sat down on the sofa, using his handkerchief as a makeshift bib as Josh munched his way through the fruit. It was rather a messy process and both of them were spattered with juice by the time the last strawberry had disappeared. Josh was starting to look sleepy by that point, but he cried when Felipe got up to take him back to his room.

He sat down again, settling the child on his knee in the hope that he would doze off. It was very quiet in the villa. Felipe felt his own eyelids drooping and blinked himself awake. However, it had been a long day and within minutes both he and Josh were fast asleep.

Becky let herself into the villa and quietly closed the front door. She paused for a moment but there was no sound coming from the nursery so she could only assume that Josh was asleep. Where Felipe had got to she had no idea, but he was probably in his study. He spent a lot of time in there of an evening, although she suspected it was less out of a desire to work than a means to escape her. Maybe he found it as difficult having her staying there as she found it being a guest in his house. She was always too aware of him to relax.

She went to the kitchen and cut herself a hunk of cheese then ate it standing at the counter. Maria had been too upset to worry about making dinner and she found herself suddenly wondering how Felipe had fared. She sighed because her conscience wouldn't allow her to let him go hungry.

She left the kitchen and went to see if he wanted her to make him an omelette, but there was no sign of him in the study when she tapped on the door. She backtracked across the hall to the sitting-room and gasped at the sight that met her.

Felipe and Josh were sprawled out on the sofa, fast asleep. Josh's clean sleepsuit was now covered in red juice and Felipe's shirt looked little better. There were red stains all down the front and it was very creased. Frankly, Becky didn't know whether to laugh or scold them because it was obvious that the pair had been up to mischief. She was still trying to decide what to do when Felipe opened one eye a crack and saw her.

He came awake with a rush, sitting up and blinking. 'I must have dozed off,' he said, his deep voice sounding even deeper with sleep.

Becky felt her stomach coil into a tight little bud and had to make a conscious effort not to react. Did he have any idea how sexy he looked, she wondered, with his black hair all rumpled and his beautiful brown eyes heavy-lidded with sleep?

'So I can see. What interests me is what you two were up to before you fell asleep.' She regarded him levelly, praying that she could keep up the pretence long enough to convince him that all she felt was annoyance because of the state Josh was in.

'Why should you think that we were up to anything?' He shot the baby a quick look and she saw a wash of colour run up his cheeks. It gave him the appearance of a small boy who had been caught doing something naughty. It was such a contrast to his usual air of being totally in control that she couldn't help staring at him.

'Ah, I see. It seems that I shall have to confess my sins, Rebecca.'

'I don't think you need to confess,' she observed with mock severity, struggling to get a grip on herself. 'The evidence speaks for itself. You two have had a strawberry feast, haven't you?'

'Guilty.' He gave her a slow smile that made his mouth curl delectably at the corners. 'But you must blame your son, not me. He is the one who ate all the strawberries. I was just his willing accomplice. Is that the right word for someone who aids and abets a criminal?'

'Criminal?' Her brows rose, although it was hard not to laugh at such nonsense. 'How can you claim that a ten-month-old baby is a criminal? He needed help to *commit* his crime!'

'Maybe he is very advanced for his age,' he suggested, completely deadpan.

'He would need to be. You're saying that he managed to get out of his cot and make his way to the kitchen. And then he opened the refrigerator door all by himself…'

'I just admitted that I was his accomplice,' he said, with a grin that made her heart melt. 'I just never realised how quick he is to learn new skills.'

'Especially when there's someone around who can teach them to him,' she shot back. 'You might be leading him down the road to ruin, Felipe, you realise?'

'Oh, I doubt if I could be blamed for doing that.'

'But I could?' Suddenly it was an effort to hold her smile. Maybe she was being overly sensitive but that comment had seemed rather too pointed. 'After all, I'm the one who teaches Josh the things he needs to know. If he doesn't turn out as you hope he will, you can lay the blame at my door, can't you, Felipe?'

'No! I never meant to imply any such thing—'

'Forget it,' she snapped, not wanting to hear any more because there was no point. She knew how he felt about her and she'd be a fool to hope that his opinion might have improved.

'Rebecca, please—'

'I told you that it doesn't matter.'

She took Josh from him, cradling the baby to her as she hurried from the room. It took only a few minutes to wash his hands and change him. Josh gave her a sleepy smile and immediately dropped off to sleep again when she laid him in his cot.

Becky moved about the room, clearing up the odds and ends she'd used, and it was only when she caught sight of herself in the mirror over the dresser that she realised she was crying.

Felipe hated her! He must do. He obviously believed that she was a bad influence on Josh and she didn't think she could bear it.

'Oh, *querida*, don't cry. Please. There is no need. This is all a silly misunderstanding.'

She hadn't heard him coming into the room and she froze when she heard his voice. When she felt his hands on her shoulders as he turned her to face him she closed her eyes because she didn't want him to see how upset she was. If Felipe knew that he had the power to hurt her, he might use it again and again...

'I am so sorry, Rebecca. Truly I am.' He drew her to him and she could feel his hands moving gently up and down her back as he tried to soothe her. 'I can't bear to see you upset like this.'

Once again his hands slid down her back and she shivered when they gently followed the curve of her spine. Felipe must have felt her tremble because his hands stilled for a moment before they moved on, only this time it felt more like he was trying to caress her than comfort her.

Becky's eyes flew open and she felt a spasm run through her when she saw the expression on his face. To see him looking at her with such hunger, such need should have shocked or scared her, but oddly enough it did neither. In some strange, inexplicable way it felt as though she had been waiting for this moment to happen all her life.

'Rebecca.'

Her name was just a whisper as it came from his lips, but it felt to her as though he had shouted it out loud. Every nerve in her body pulsed with the sound of it, trembled because of the way he had said it. When he bent towards her she was already moving towards him so that their mouths met with a small jolt.

Becky clung to him as her head spun, feeling the solidness of his body beneath her hands. He was still wearing the rumpled shirt and she could feel the heat of his skin flowing through her palms. The delicate scent of crushed strawberries mingled with the scent of his body to create a musky perfume that stirred her unbearably so that her senses seemed to be far more acute than normal.

She could hear the rasp of his breathing, the whisper of hers, feel his heart beating and hers trying to match its rhythm; she could taste the heady flavour of him when he opened his mouth and let his tongue slide inside hers...

Becky gave a sharp, little moan, unable to hold back when she felt his tongue tracing the outline of her lips. Their mouths were barely touching yet it was the most sensually stirring experience she'd ever had. She could feel Felipe's tongue following the curve of her upper lip, feel her breath catch when it paused while he enjoyed its shape and taste a moment longer, feel the ripple that ran through her when it moved on. By the time he reached her lower lip and gently drew it into his mouth, she was trembling. It seemed the most natural thing in the world when he slowly backed her up against the wall and let his weight settle against her so that she could feel the hard evidence of his desire.

'Feel what you do to me, *querida*?' he whispered, his breath warm on her skin as his mouth glided over her jaw and down her throat.

Becky moaned when she felt little pools of heat collecting beneath her skin wherever his lips had touched. 'Yes,' she whispered huskily, unable to manage more than the single word.

His lips glided back up her throat, found her mouth again, treated her to another drugging kiss. And all the time desire was building inside her, growing stronger with each second that passed. Each touch of his hands made her tremble, each kiss made her burn, each beat of her heart and his made their passion for each other grow stronger.

What was happening was unlike anything she'd experienced with Antonio. She had loved Antonio very much, but her feelings for Felipe were far more complex. Felipe had the power to hurt her on so many different levels if she wasn't careful.

He must have felt her tense because his hands and mouth suddenly stilled. Becky heard him draw in a rasping breath before he pulled away from her. Just for a moment there was a blaze of passion in his eyes that made her ache to have him take her back in his arms. Then it was gone and she saw the bitter self-reproach that had replaced it.

'I apologise, Rebecca. That should never have happened.'

He turned and strode out of the room and she heard his bedroom door close a moment later. Becky stood where she was, feeling desire growing cold inside her. She had seen the regret in Felipe's eyes and knew that he would never forgive himself for what had happened. Maybe he wouldn't forgive her for causing it either. After all, he had come within a hairsbreadth of making love to her, the woman he despised.

Her eyes filled with tears again. If the situation had been bad before, it could only get worse.

He couldn't believe he had done that!

Felipe paced his room, but there was no way he could ease the agony he felt. He had almost made love to Rebecca...

Hell, he *had* made love to her! Why should he spare himself when the truth had to be faced? He had kissed and caressed her in the most intimate way, and even though technically they hadn't made love it had felt as though they had. He'd felt more while he'd been kissing her than he'd felt after spending a whole night in bed with another woman.

The thought brought him up short. Kissing Rebecca had felt more wonderful than making love even to Teresa. With Rebecca he hadn't been able to keep any part of him separate. His whole being—everything he was—had been caught up by the need to love her. If he hadn't felt her withdrawal, who knew what might have happened? But it was the reason why she had drawn back that caused him such pain.

Had Rebecca suddenly thought about Antonio? And had she been ashamed of what they'd been doing?

He swore softly. He was too experienced not to know that she'd been with him every step of the way, that her desire had been just as great as his. But had it been right to make her feel like that? Was it right to want her this way? She was the mother of his brother's son, the woman Antonio had loved, and he had been making love to her.

He doubted if he could have felt more wretched as he was assailed by guilt. What made it even worse was knowing that Rebecca was probably in her room at that very moment, torturing herself with the thought of how she had betrayed Antonio.

She had no need to blame herself, though. She was still a young woman with her whole life ahead of her. Even though she had loved Antonio, she couldn't live on her memories for ever. Antonio wouldn't have wanted her to—he knew that without the shadow of a doubt. Antonio would have wanted Rebecca to be happy.

The thought seemed to wash away his guilt and it no longer felt as though he needed to reproach himself. Antonio would have wanted only the best for Rebecca and Josh, that they would be loved and cared for, cherished. Maybe he was being presumptuous, but all of a sudden Felipe knew that he wanted to be the one to care for them. The question was, would Rebecca let him? Would she trust him to help her, tell him why she was afraid?

She might if he was honest with her, a small voice inside his head suggested, and he laughed.

Why on earth hadn't he thought of doing that before? He knew in his heart that she hadn't used Antonio for his money, that everything she had done had been with the very best of intentions, so maybe it was time he told *her* that.

His heart lifted. He would talk to Rebecca in the morning, tell her how he felt then ask her to tell him the truth. No matter what this secret was that she was keeping from him, it couldn't be *that* bad. They would find a way to work it out, he and Rebecca.

Together.

Becky was up before six and had Josh washed and dressed a short time later. She took him into the kitchen and let him crawl around the floor while she made him some breakfast.

He was still a little unsteady and kept going backwards instead of forwards, but he would soon get the hang of it. In another few weeks he would be walking and talking, growing from a baby into an inquisitive little boy. She only hoped that she would be around to watch him growing up, but there were no guarantees. Not after last night and what had happened. Felipe might use it as the perfect excuse to get rid of her.

A sob caught in her throat but she refused to cry. Tears weren't going to help. She had to face what she had done and deal with the repercussions it was bound to cause.

She picked up Josh and put him in his high chair then helped him spoon cereal into his mouth. He was at the stage of wanting to do everything himself so mealtimes were rather messy affairs. She was just wiping up a dollop of cereal that had ended up on the floor when she looked up and saw Felipe standing in the doorway, watching her.

'*Buenos dias,*' he said politely, coming into the room and pausing beside Josh's chair to ruffle his hair.

'Good morning,' she replied, praying that he couldn't hear the strain in her voice. She finished cleaning up the mess then went to the sink to rinse out the cloth, glancing round when Felipe reached for the coffee-pot on the counter beside her.

'Would you like coffee, Rebecca?' he asked in the same perfectly polite tone, which was starting to grate on her nerves.

'If you're having some,' she said equally politely, then felt herself flush when she caught the amused look he gave her.

Turning, she took a towel off the rack, dried her hands then went to get Josh a banana. She sliced it up and put it in a dish, taking her time because she wasn't sure how to handle the situation. Should she mention what had happened last night, or wait and see if Felipe brought it up?

'I'm making toast—would you like some as well?'

She jumped when he spoke, casting an uncertain glance over her shoulder at him. He was slicing bread to go in the toaster and he smiled calmly at her. 'You really should eat something, Rebecca. You didn't have any dinner last night and you must be hungry.'

'I'll have a slice if you're making some,' she said quickly, afraid that mention of dinner would lead to other topics.

She took a deep breath as he turned to put the bread in the toaster, trying to blot out the images that filled her mind. It would serve no purpose recalling how his mouth had felt when he'd kissed her, how his hands had caressed her, how his skin had smelled...

Josh knocked his dish onto the floor and Becky jumped. She bent to pick it up, but her hands were trembling so much that it was an effort to make them obey her. Slippery bits of banana slid through her fingers and she bit her lip in dismay.

'Let me do that.'

Felipe gently grasped her shoulders and helped her to her feet, and she was shocked by the tenderness in his eyes. He quickly cleared up the mess and wiped Josh's sticky fingers then lifted him out of his chair and put him on the floor.

Becky looked round uncertainly, feeling at a loss to know what to do. Felipe seemed to have taken charge, making her superfluous. When he placed a cup of coffee on the breakfast bar, along with a plate of buttered toast, she automatically sat down.

He poured himself a cup of coffee and sat beside her, and she flinched when his arm brushed hers. All of a sudden the tension in the kitchen was palpable. She could feel it and knew that he could, too.

'What happened last night wasn't planned, Rebecca.'

His voice was perfectly level so that for a moment she didn't realise what he meant. She felt a wash of colour run up her face when it sank in. She doubted if she could have sounded so matter-of-fact, but maybe he found it easier to deal with the thought of them making love than she did. It was an effort to keep her mind focused when he continued in the same even tone.

'Nevertheless, I do not regret that it happened. In fact, I'm glad that it did because it has helped me see this situation far more clearly.'

She looked at him, unable to hide her surprise. 'What do you mean?'

'That I've been wrong about you, Rebecca.' He shrugged but she could see a nerve beating in his jaw and realised that he was nowhere near as calm as he was pretending to be. 'You aren't who I thought you were.'

'I don't know what you expect me to say,' she said hoarsely. The statement had come like a bolt from the blue and she had no idea how to react. 'You had formed your own opinion of me before we even met.'

'I know. And now I realise that I was completely wrong about you.'

His voice was so gentle that she couldn't find it in her to resist when he turned her to face him. 'I know in my heart that you aren't the scheming, mercenary woman I thought you to be. I apologise for having thought that of you in the first place.'

His fingers brushed the soft skin under her jaw and she shivered because it had triggered memories of the night before. It was an effort to focus on what he was saying when he continued in the same butter-soft tone.

'You are a kind and caring woman, a loving mother to Josh and a skilled nurse. I know all that now, Rebecca, and I admit that I was wrong. What I don't understand is why you let me believe the worst when you could have told me the truth. What are you hiding from me?'

Felipe held his breath. Would Rebecca find the courage to tell him? Would she open her heart and share this dreadful secret with him so that he could help her?

He had barely slept with worrying about it, but he didn't dare let her see how important it was to him. He had to make her trust him, had to make her understand that he wouldn't do anything to hurt her. All of a sudden that seemed more important than anything. She had suffered enough and she shouldn't be allowed to endure any more.

'I…I don't know what you mean,' she began, then stopped and swallowed.

He heard the dry click of her throat and his heart ached because of what she must be going through. It was obvious how afraid she was and he wished with all his heart that he could think of a way to make this easier for her, but there was nothing he could do. He had taken the first step and she had to take the next all by herself.

'I'm glad you realise that I never deceived Antonio,' she said at last with a catch in her voice. 'I loved him too much to hurt him.'

Felipe's heart contracted on a spasm of pain. Even though it made him feel awful to admit it, it hurt to hear her say how much she had loved his brother. It was an effort to keep the ache out of his voice, but he couldn't and wouldn't put her under any more pressure.

'And I know how much Antonio loved you because he told me in his last letter.' He sighed when he saw the sadness in her beautiful eyes. 'I chose to ignore that and believe only what I wanted to believe, but now I want to know the truth. What haven't you told me? Has it something to do with Josh?'

He knew he was right the moment he saw panic flare in her eyes. This secret Rebecca was keeping concerned his nephew,

but for the life of him he couldn't imagine what it was. The
boy was obviously Antonio's son so that couldn't be the problem…

She suddenly pushed back her chair and stood up. Bending,
she scooped Josh up into her arms. Her face was set into tight
lines that hinted at the strain she was under, but she faced him
squarely.

'You're imagining things, Felipe.' She shrugged but he'd
seen the tremor that had raced through her slender body and
knew that she was lying. 'I'm not keeping anything from you.'

He stood up abruptly, knowing that it was pointless trying
to press her at the moment. She was too afraid to tell him the
truth even after what had happened between them last night…

Maybe *because* of what had happened, a small voice inside
him whispered. Maybe she regretted those minutes she had
spent in his arms, and it was that which was causing her such
distress now.

Felipe felt a knifing pain run through him at the thought.
The last thing he wanted was to cause her any more distress,
but there was little he could do about it. Rebecca had to deal
with her feelings for Antonio in her own time—if she ever
learned to deal with them, of course.

It was an effort not to show how much that idea upset him,
but there was no way that he would add to her anguish. 'Then
there is nothing more to be said on the subject, is there?'

He gave her a gentle smile but his heart felt like lead. Had
he been a fool to imagine that she'd responded to *him* last
night? Maybe the true explanation was that he had been merely
a substitute for his brother. Had Rebecca pretended that it had
been Antonio holding her in his arms, Antonio who'd been
kissing her?

'It will not be possible for you to work with Maria not being
here to look after Josh,' he told her, amazed that his voice
sounded so normal when it felt as though he had been dealt
the most horrendous blow. 'I shall inform your colleagues not
to expect you today.'

She shook her head. 'No, don't do that. I'll take Josh to the crèche. He will enjoy being with the other children for a change.'

'If that is what you wish to do. The staff who work in the crèche are all highly trained.'

'I know. Like everyone else who works at the Clinica Valdez.'

'I wanted only the best when I opened the clinic,' he said flatly. 'The best staff, the best facilities, the best of everything.'

'And you've achieved all that. It's a wonderful place, Felipe. You must have worked very hard to set it up,' she said softly.

'*Sí.*' He shrugged but he couldn't deny the hollow feeling it gave him to realise how much of his life had been spent achieving his dream. Would he do the same again if he was given the same choices? Once he would have said yes, of course he would, but now he was no longer certain.

It scared him to have to face that fact. If he didn't have his work, what did he have that meant anything to him? Maybe it was that thought which made him open his heart when it should have been the last thing he did right then.

'It was my dream to one day open my own hospital, but it came at a price. It left me with very little time for a personal life.'

'And you regret that?' she asked, as though his answer really mattered to her.

'Yes. By now I might have had a wife and family if I hadn't devoted so much of my time to the Clinica Valdez.'

'At least you have Josh,' she said with a catch in her voice which made his heart ache even more. Even now she was worried about him, cared how he felt. It was both a pleasure and a pain to realise it, to know once again how wrong he had been about her in the beginning.

'Only for as long as you choose to remain here.' He took a deep breath but there was no way that he could lie to her now. 'If you decide to leave, I can't stop you, Rebecca. After all, you are the child's mother.'

'Yes,' she said hollowly. 'I'm his mother.'

She turned to leave but he'd seen the fear that had flared in her eyes once again. Felipe frowned as he heard her footsteps crossing the hall. He was convinced that whatever she was hiding from him had to do with Josh, but what was it? What was this dreadful secret that she was too scared to tell him?

He knew that he wouldn't rest until he'd found out the truth. Maybe Rebecca could never be anything more to him than the mother of his brother's child, but he needed to solve this last piece of the puzzle.

CHAPTER TEN

'HE JUST opened his eyes and said, "I'm thirsty, Mum." I couldn't believe it!'

'I'm so pleased for you both!' Becky hugged Diane and Tim Palmer then laughed as she wiped a tear from her eyes. 'I don't know why we're crying when we should be celebrating!'

Ryan had suddenly awoken from his coma that morning. Felipe was with him at the moment, running some tests. Silvia Ramirez had told her that a neurologist was flying out from Madrid that afternoon to carry out more tests, but so far the signs were encouraging.

'Does this mean that we'll be able to take Ryan home soon?' Diane demanded eagerly.

'Hopefully, although you might need to stay a while longer just to make sure that he's stable,' Becky warned, sitting down beside Diane on the sofa.

They were using the relatives' suite—a comfortable little apartment attached to the children's department. Diane and Tim had been staying there ever since Ryan had been admitted to the hospital. Becky found herself thinking that Felipe had thought of everything when he'd had the plans drawn up for the Clinica Valdez.

The thought naturally reminded her of what had happened that morning and she sighed because it was hard to recall the sadness in his voice when he'd spoken about the emptiness of his life. She'd never imagined that she would feel such sympathy for him, although sympathy wasn't the only thing she felt.

Heat rushed through her as she recalled the way he'd kissed her. Even though he'd appeared to regret it afterwards, it didn't change what had happened. It had made it even more difficult to deal with his searching questions that morning. She longed to tell him the truth, but how could she take that risk?

Felipe had told her he'd revised his opinion of her, but how would he feel if he found out that she wasn't Josh's real mother? His views could change again and the fear that he might try to take Josh away from her couldn't be quietened.

It was an effort to put aside such worrying thoughts when Tim asked her about the tests that were being carried out on his son. Becky explained that Ryan's responses to various stimuli would be tested to ascertain that his brain was functioning properly. The child's basic responses such as breathing, yawning, coughing and swallowing had been fine all along, so there was obviously no damage to his brain stem. However, there might be damage to other areas.

Diane and Tim listened intently, asking questions whenever they didn't understand. Becky didn't go into too much detail about the problems they might face in the future because it would be best if the neurologist completed his assessment first. Physical and mental disability couldn't be ruled out at this stage, but there was no point worrying them unnecessarily. However, by the time Felipe arrived, they were beginning to realise that Ryan wasn't completely out of the woods yet.

He smiled as he sat down. 'Ryan is asking for you, but before you go back to see him I just wanted to say that the signs are very encouraging. Obviously, my colleague, Dr Menendez, is the expert in this field, but we're hopeful that there is no serious brain damage.'

Becky heaved a sigh of relief as Diane and Tim left, looking a lot happier. 'Thank heavens for that! It's been such a worrying time for them.'

'It has.' He smiled and she felt heat ripple along her veins when she saw the warmth in his eyes. When had he started looking at her like that? she wondered. Since last night? She'd thought he'd regretted what had happened but maybe—just maybe—she'd been wrong.

'Silvia told me that you offered to give up your break and

talk to them while we carried out the tests on Ryan,' he said quietly. 'Thank you.'

'It's what I'm paid to do,' she replied, quickly standing up. She couldn't afford to let herself be distracted by the thought. She had to remember what a dangerous situation she was in. It would take very little to uncover her secret.

'No, you are paid to care for the children we treat here. Giving support to the parents is something you do out of the goodness of your heart, Rebecca.'

There was a grating note in his voice when he said that, and she sighed. 'I didn't think you believed that I had a heart.'

He looked at her with a searching light in his eyes. 'I told you this morning that I knew I was wrong about you.'

She half expected him to say something else, maybe bring up the subject of why she had allowed him to continue thinking so badly of her, but surprisingly he didn't pursue it. 'So how was Josh when you left him at the crèche?'

'Fine. He was very excited because he could see all the other children.' She summoned a smile, not wanting him to see how relieved she felt because it would only arouse his curiosity. 'He barely spared me a glance when I left, in fact.'

'He is a credit to you, Rebecca. The fact that he is happy to be left with strangers proves how secure he feels.'

'Thank you.' She was deeply touched by the comment. 'All I ever wanted was for him to be safe and happy.'

'I realise that. Everything you have done has been for his sake. And for Antonio's sake, of course. It must mean a lot to you to take care of his son.'

'Do you really believe that?' she said urgently. If she could believe what he'd said then maybe she could risk telling him the truth after all?

'*Claro que sí*. Of course,' he said flatly, and her heart sank when she heard the reservation in his voice.

'But? There was a definite *but* tagged onto the end of that, Felipe, wasn't there?'

'Perhaps.' He sighed. 'Sometimes people do things in good faith and end up causing themselves a great many problems. I only hope that your desire to look after Josh hasn't caused you to do something you now regret.'

'I did what had to be done and I would do exactly the same thing all over again,' she said flatly, because it was true. No matter how difficult the situation was or how much anguish it caused her personally, she didn't regret the decisions she'd made.

'Then I hope that one day you will trust me enough to tell me the truth, Rebecca. Like you, my only concern is Josh's welfare.'

Becky sensed that he was hurt by her refusal to tell him the whole story, but she still wasn't sure that he would understand. She heard Felipe sigh when she remained silent.

'It would be best if we left this conversation until another time. Work isn't the place to discuss it.' He turned to leave then paused and glanced back. 'Before I forget, I shall be out this evening so you will have the villa to yourself. Dr Menendez and I are old friends and I have invited him out for dinner. It will give us a chance to catch up on what has been happening.'

'Oh, right. Thank you for letting me know.' She shrugged when he looked quizzically at her. 'I was going to make dinner for us both, but I won't need to bother now.'

'I do not expect you to cook for me because you are living under my roof, Rebecca.'

'I never imagined that you did. However, with Maria being away, it seemed more sensible to make a meal for us both.'

She could feel the colour rushing up her face and turned to plump up the cushions on the sofa. Did Felipe think that she was trying to ingratiate herself even further by offering to cook him a meal?

'I'm sorry. I did not mean that the way it sounded.' He sighed when she shot him a startled look. 'I am not used to having to think before I speak, I'm afraid. There has never been anyone to question me before.'

'Before me, you mean?' She gave a light laugh, hoping it didn't sound as strained to him as it did to her. 'You must be sorry you met me, Felipe. I've done nothing but disrupt your life, have I?'

'You have turned everything on its head, Rebecca, although I am not sorry about it.'

'What do you mean?' she demanded, startled.

'That maybe my life needed to be disrupted before I could see what was missing from it. I don't regret meeting you, Rebecca. If there is anything I regret, it's that we didn't meet before.'

Before Antonio.

The words hung between them, unspoken yet clear all the same. Becky felt her heart pound when she looked into his eyes and saw the expression they held. There was regret in them but it was mingled with another emotion which made her body burn with a sudden intense heat. To know that Felipe still wanted her that morning as he had wanted her the night before made her feel as though the bottom had just dropped out of her world.

It was a relief when he abruptly left the room because she had no idea what she might have said. Her head seemed to be whirling. Felipe had admitted that his opinion of her had undergone a complete reversal, but so, too, had her opinion of him. The idea terrified her.

If he was no longer her enemy, how much more difficult was it going to be to keep her secret from him? Could you love someone and keep a part of yourself separate?

The thought slid into her mind and she gasped. Was she falling in love with Felipe? Was it possible? She wanted to deny it, but it wasn't possible to do that.

Not after last night.

Why on earth had he said that?

Felipe bit back a groan as he went into his office. He sat down behind his desk, automatically reaching for the pile of letters his secretary had left for him to sign. He stared at the beautifully printed pages without seeing a word that was written on them. He kept hearing himself telling Rebecca that he regretted not having met her *before* she'd met Antonio.

He pushed back his chair and paced the room, too on edge to sit still. She had understood what he'd meant even though he'd managed to stop himself saying his brother's name. He'd seen the shock in her eyes and the awareness that had followed it. And yet she hadn't looked as though the idea had sickened her. He'd had the definite impression that she wished the same thing, in fact. But if that was the case, why was she so reluctant to tell him the truth? Just how bad was this secret she was keeping?

He groaned again. The harder he tried to understand the situation, the more difficult it became. Frankly, there was a danger that it would drive him insane if he didn't find out the truth soon. Maybe it was time he did just that. It didn't feel right to go behind Rebecca's back, but he had no choice. If she wouldn't tell him, someone else would!

Picking up the phone, he dialled the London office of the firm of solicitors his brother had used. He'd had little contact with them since the funeral, but maybe it was time he started asking some questions. The solicitor who had handled Antonio's affairs was in court that day so Felipe left a message asking the man to get back to him and hung up.

Picking up the letters, he tried to concentrate, but it was impossible to keep his mind on the task. Finding out the truth about Rebecca seemed far more important than the smooth running of the Clinica Valdez. It scared him to death to have to admit it.

All of a sudden it felt as though there were no longer any guidelines in his life. He was drifting through time and space with no idea what would happen next. All he could do was hope that he wouldn't regret discovering Rebecca's secret. It could prove to be a big mistake, but it was a risk he had to take.

Until he knew what Rebecca was hiding, he couldn't make any plans for their future. Whether he liked the idea or not, the two were intrinsically linked.

* * *

It was a busy afternoon. They had several new admissions to the children's ward so Becky was kept busy dealing with them. One child in particular was giving cause for concern.

Four-year-old Christopher Thomas was suffering from hyperpyrexia, a severe form of heatstroke. He had been playing in the sun and had suffered quite extensive sunburn to his back and shoulders. Becky got him settled then went to have a word with his parents.

'Christopher's temperature is coming down but he's still quite poorly,' she explained. 'The staff in Casualty managed to cool him by wrapping him in a wet sheet and using a fan. However, we shall need to keep him on a drip overnight to replace all the fluids he's lost.'

'He will be all right, won't he?' Elaine Thomas demanded. 'We had no idea he was ill until one of the reps from the hotel came to fetch us.'

'He wasn't with you?' Becky asked in surprise.

'No, we left him at the children's club. I mean, that's the whole point of going on holiday, isn't it?' Michael Thomas, the child's father, put in belligerently. 'You can offload the kids and have some time to yourself. Elaine and I were in the bar when that girl who runs the club came to find us.'

'So have you any idea how long Christopher was out in the sun?' Becky asked.

'A couple of hours, I suppose. He was at the kids' club all morning then we told him to stay by the pool after that. Elaine and I always go to the bar at lunchtime and he's such a nuisance if we take him with us, all the time asking if he can go and play,' Michael told her. 'Of course, I blame the staff for what's happened. They should have been keeping an eye on him, shouldn't they? That's what they're paid to do. I wouldn't mind but I'd just ordered a round of drinks and we had to leave them to bring him here because that rep insisted.'

Becky managed to hide her dismay. It was hard to imagine how any father could be more concerned about a drink than his child's welfare. 'It's a good job you did bring him straight to the clinic, Mr Thomas. Christopher was very ill when he was admitted. Not to put too fine a point on it, he could have died.'

She gave the parents a moment to digest that, hoping it would stop them being so careless in the future. Heatstroke was far more serious than people realised. Once the body lost its ability to cool itself, its core temperature rose dramatically. It wasn't unknown for people to die from severe heatstroke, especially a child of Christopher's age.

'Anyway, I'll take you in to see him now. He's been sick and he might be a little disorientated, but by tomorrow he should be feeling much better. We'll keep him in overnight to monitor his condition.'

'We won't have to stay, will we?' Michael demanded. 'I mean, this is a proper hospital, isn't it? There'll be nurses here to look after him?'

'Of course. The Clinica Valdez is one of the biggest hospitals on the island,' she assured him. 'But I'm sure Christopher would prefer it if you were to stay with him. It really isn't a problem as far as we're concerned, I assure you. There's a family suite that you can use.'

'Maybe it's not a problem for you, but it's a problem for us. We've booked to go on a trip tonight and they won't refund our money if we cancel at the last minute.' Michael turned to his wife. 'There's not much point in us staying here, is there, Elaine?'

'Well, I suppose not,' she agreed hesitantly. She gave Becky a watery smile. 'So long as you're sure Christopher will be properly looked after, of course.'

'Christopher will receive the very best care,' she said shortly, not trusting herself to say too much.

She led the couple into the room and left them there. How long they would stay was anyone's guess. Frankly, she found it hard to believe that people could be so callous, although she could easily imagine Tara leaving Josh in a hospital on his own while she went off to enjoy herself.

The thought made her see that she'd been right to come to Mallorca. Making sure that Josh was safe was the only thing that mattered. It would be marvellous if she could tell Felipe the truth, of course, but it was too dangerous.

She couldn't afford to let her feelings for him overrule common sense. Deep down she knew that Felipe would have a hard time accepting that she had lied to him about being Josh's mother. He might never be able to forgive her for deceiving him. She might not only lose Josh but Felipe's support as well.

Her heart ached at the thought.

Becky collected Josh from the crèche at the end of the day and took him back to the villa. It felt strange, letting herself in to the empty house. Normally Maria would have come bustling out to meet her, telling her all about the things Josh had done while she'd been at work.

She took him into the kitchen and gave him some wooden spoons to play with while she made them something to eat. They both had scrambled eggs, with toast soldiers for Josh, and strawberries to follow. She wiped his hands and face then lifted him out of his high chair and kissed him.

'Not as much fun as when your Uncle Felipe gave you those strawberries last night, was it, poppet?'

Josh bounced up and down in her arms, seeming to react to the name, or maybe it was she who had reacted to it. Just saying Felipe's name out loud had sent a thrill coursing through her, made her skin tingle and her breath catch. It made her realise just how difficult it was going to be, living under the same roof as this man without letting him see how she felt.

It was a sobering thought and it stayed with her the whole time she was getting Josh ready for bed. He was worn out after his day in the crèche and could hardly keep his eyes open while she was bathing him. She laid him in his cot and wound up the clockwork mobile that hung from the ceiling so that he could watch the plastic fishes and dolphins bobbing around while he fell asleep.

It had just gone seven when she went into the sitting room and found herself wondering how to fill in the hours until it was time for bed. Although Felipe rarely spent any time with her once they'd finished dinner, she had never felt lonely. Just knowing that he was in the house had always seemed to be enough.

Becky sighed because that thought simply reinforced all her earlier ones about her feelings for him. It was worrying to think that she was falling in love with him when there was no future for them. Unless she told him the truth about Josh there was no chance of their relationship developing.

Her heart felt unusually heavy as she wandered out onto the terrace and stared across the bay. The sun was riding low in the sky, turning the sea blood-red where the last dying rays touched it. It had been extremely hot all day and the temperature hadn't dropped very much. She would have loved a dip in the pool, but she didn't like to stray too far from the house in case Josh woke up. She was just about to go back inside when she heard footsteps coming along the path and gasped when Felipe appeared.

'What are you doing here? I thought you were going out to dinner with your friend?'

'I was, but Ramon decided to catch the early flight back to Madrid. He has a busy day tomorrow and needed time to prepare for it.' Felipe summoned a smile, hoping that Rebecca wouldn't question him about his change of plans. Did he really want her to find out that it had been *he* who had cut short the evening and not Ramon Menendez?

He knew that Ramon had been looking forward to the evening, but as the afternoon had passed he'd found himself growing increasingly reluctant about their proposed dinner. In the end he'd cancelled their arrangements, using the excuse that something urgent had cropped up at the clinic.

Ramon had accepted it without question, used to having his own plans disrupted by the demands of the job. However, Felipe wasn't as confident that Rebecca would believe him, and it was the thought of her guessing that he hadn't been able to stand being apart from her for a whole evening that made him feel so uncomfortable.

'What a shame!' she exclaimed. 'You were looking forward to it, too.'

'I was. But these things happen so there is no point worrying about them,' he said, feeling worse because she was obviously disappointed for him.

'I suppose so. Anyway, are you hungry? You must be if you've missed out on dinner,' she continued, and he felt himself relax when he realised that she'd accepted his story.

'Not really,' he replied truthfully. 'It's so hot tonight that I think I would prefer a swim rather than a meal.'

'I was just wishing I could go for a swim,' she said wistfully. She shrugged when he looked quizzically at her. 'I didn't want to miss hearing Josh if he woke up so I thought it best not to go as far as the pool.'

'You could move the baby alarm onto the patio,' he suggested, thinking how typical it was of her to put the baby's welfare first. He felt a little flurry of pleasure run through him because it was proof that he had no need to worry what the solicitor might tell him. How could there be anything bad to say about Rebecca when he could see for himself what kind of a woman she was?

'Why didn't I think of that?' she exclaimed, laughing. 'I suppose I'm not used to having a baby alarm. There wasn't much need for one when Josh and I were sharing a bedroom, but it's the perfect solution.'

'Good. I'm glad that is settled.'

Felipe smiled back because her delight was so contagious. He followed her back inside while they got changed, parting company in the hall to go to their respective bedrooms. Rebecca's door was closed when he passed it a few minutes later so he didn't wait for her. He didn't want her to think that he was too eager to spend the evening with her.

He sighed as he made his way down to the pool. He couldn't lie to himself, though. Just the thought of having a few hours alone with her was making his blood heat, but he had to control himself. Until he'd cleared up the last little question about what she was hiding from him he had to keep his emotions in check.

It was something he'd never had any difficulty doing in the past, but as he slid into the water he knew it was going to be a struggle. It was hard to resist temptation when it came in the form of Rebecca.

Felipe was already in the pool by the time Becky arrived. He had switched on the perimeter lights and the water was the most glorious shade of azure blue. He swam over to the side and smiled up at her.

'The water is wonderful. Not too hot and not too cool.'

'Oh, good.'

She summoned a smile but it wasn't easy to control the surge her pulse gave. It was the first time she had seen him wearing swimming trunks and he was an arresting sight. His body was firm and well muscled, the thick dark hair that covered his chest arrowing down and disappearing into the waistband of his black trunks.

She felt incredibly self-conscious as she pulled her T-shirt over her head and dropped it on the grass. She could feel him watching her as she sat on the side of the pool, and wished that she had something more glamorous to wear than the modest blue swimsuit which she had bought from a local charity shop. It was a relief to slide into the water and hide herself from view, although the coolness of it took her breath away.

'I thought you said it wasn't cold!'

'It isn't. It only feels that way because you are so hot.' He smiled at her, his eyes playing over her face before they dropped to her body.

Becky felt a shiver run through her that owed itself less to the chilly water than to the intent scrutiny he was subjecting her to. And yet when his eyes came back to her face they were so full of warmth that she was instantly flooded with heat again. There wasn't a doubt in her mind that he'd liked what he'd seen, unglamorous swimsuit notwithstanding.

She ducked under the water, afraid that he would guess how that made her feel. It helped to cool her down, probably too much, because she was shivering when she surfaced.

Felipe frowned when he saw her shiver. 'You really are cold. Come, I shall race you to the other end of the pool. That will help you to warm up.'

'You're on,' she agreed, and swam as fast as she could to the other end. She was halfway there when she realised that Felipe was swimming alongside her, although he made no attempt to overtake her. She caught hold of the handrail, dragging in a lungful of air because she was so out of breath although Felipe wasn't even breathing hard.

'You let me win. You could easily have beaten me if you'd tried.'

'Perhaps. But at least it helped you to warm up, didn't it, Rebecca?' He gave her a quick smile then dived under the water and swam to the opposite end of the pool.

Becky sighed as she set off at a more sedate pace. There was no doubt that his attitude towards her had undergone a massive change, but could she be sure that he would understand if she told him the truth about Josh? She was tempted, very tempted, but she needed to be sure that she was doing the right thing.

The thought stayed with her as she swam up and down the pool. She wasn't a strong swimmer so she turned onto her back after a couple of lengths and let herself drift. Night was drawing in and the sky was turning black. The garden was secluded and there was little noise beyond the faint drone of traffic passing along the main road.

It was soothing to float in the water and she gradually felt herself relax. Maybe she was making things too difficult. Maybe she should stop looking for problems and trust her instincts…

'Come, Rebecca, we have been in the water quite long enough. I would not like you to catch a chill.'

She jumped when Felipe appeared beside her, beating at the water in sudden panic when she felt herself starting to sink. He put his arms around her and drew her against him, supporting her while she got her breath back.

'I'm sorry,' he said contritely. 'I didn't mean to scare you.'

'I didn't realise I was in the deep end,' she murmured, because it was impossible to form the words any more clearly.

She took another breath as the water lapped around them but it did very little to help. Felipe needed to kick his legs to keep them both afloat, and each time she felt his muscular thighs touching hers a little more air escaped from her body instead of entering it.

'You were daydreaming,' he said softly, his deep voice sounding oddly strained. He kicked once again and she stiffened when she felt his hips brushing hers this time, felt the way his body responded immediately to the contact. Her eyes rose to his face and she knew that he could see the awareness they held.

'Felipe…'

'No. Don't say anything. There is no need because I understand how you feel. Or I hope I do.' His smile was tender and oddly hesitant, as though he was no longer sure about anything any more.

It touched her to know that this proud, confident man could have doubts. At that moment all she wanted to do was reassure him, make him understand that she had never set out to hurt him, yet there wasn't any way to do that unless she told him the truth, and that was the one thing she couldn't do. Not yet. It was that last thought which prompted her to do what she did next.

She slid her arms around his neck and pulled his head down so that she could kiss him. There was a moment when she felt him tense, when she wondered if he would resist, and then he was bending towards her. Their mouths met softly then drew apart. Becky could feel her heart drumming and knew that he could feel it, too, but there was nothing she could do about it.

The water lapped around them, pushing them together then drawing them apart, and it was the sweetest kind of torment to feel his body, so hard and strong, brushing against hers. When Felipe removed one hand from her waist and placed it gently at the side of her neck so that he could tilt her face up, she shuddered and felt the answering ripple that ran through him.

She gave a sharp little moan when she felt his lips closing over hers and tasted their sweetness, their coolness. And yet beneath the chill caused by the water there was heat, such heat that it seemed to flare along her veins and burn her up until it felt as though her whole body was consumed by it.

He dragged his mouth away from hers and his eyes were filled with such passion that she started shivering uncontrollably despite the heat that was flowing through her limbs. 'I want you so much, Rebecca, but I will not do anything you don't want me to do. Tell me to stop if that is what you want.'

'It...it isn't.' Her voice barely carried above the sound of the water slapping against the sides of the pool. She swallowed hard, feeling the knot of tension and desire clogging her throat. 'I don't want you to stop, Felipe. Please.'

He gave a rough little laugh as he pulled her to him, his hands firm on her hips as he held her against him and let her feel his desire for her. 'Then your wish shall be granted, *querida*.'

Becky clung to him as passion rose and swelled inside her again just as the water swelled around them. When she felt his hands sliding up her body she bit her lip then gasped when she felt his fingers move inside the cups of her swimsuit and brush her nipples. When he suddenly lifted her up in the water and placed his mouth to the taut little buds she closed her eyes.

Every bit of her seemed to be consumed by what was happening as wave after wave of sensation flowed through her, weakening her limbs, making her tremble. When he let her slide back down into the water and into his arms, she couldn't have kept herself afloat if he hadn't been holding her. It took her a moment before she realised that he was speaking.

'I'm sorry....?'

'Josh is crying. Listen.'

Becky took a deep breath as she heard the thin little wail coming from the speaker she had set up on the patio. 'I...I'd better go and see if he's all right.'

'*Sí*.' Felipe kept his arms around her waist and his eyes were very dark as he looked at her, full of tenderness. 'Do you need help to swim to the steps, Rebecca?'

'I… No. Thank you. I can manage.'

She summoned a smile but the speed with which everything had happened had shocked her. How could she have let it happen again after last night? How could Felipe, because he had been just as willing a participant in what had gone on. His passion had been equally great as hers had been.

The thought sent a tremor coursing through her. It took every scrap of strength she possessed to swim to the steps and climb out of the pool. Dragging on her T-shirt, she hurried into the villa and went to check on Josh.

He was hot and thirsty so she sponged him down and changed him, then gave him a drink of water. He was still a little fretful so she took him into her room and laid him on her bed while she changed out of the wet swimsuit into her night-dress.

Picking him up again, she carried him to the window and looked out across the darkened gardens. The pool lights were still on and as she watched she saw Felipe getting out of the water. For a moment he was caught in the glow from the lights and she felt her heart catch as she looked at him standing there, so tall and strong, so handsome and desirable.

She wanted him so much that it was like a fever in her blood. She wanted to run outside and pour out the whole story, trust that he would understand so that they could find the happiness she knew could be theirs. She'd seen how he'd looked at her, felt how he'd wanted her, *knew* that they could have something so wonderful, so magical that it would last the whole of their lives and beyond.

She wanted to tell him the truth, but she didn't dare.

CHAPTER ELEVEN

'AND there was a phone call from the Clinica Rosada, Dr Valdez. The director was expecting you to call him yesterday to finalise the arrangements for the conference next month.'

'I'm afraid I forgot.' Felipe saw the surprise in his secretary's eyes and bit back a sigh. It simply wasn't like him to forget anything that concerned his work so it was no wonder she was shocked.

He picked up his diary, not wanting to dwell on the reason he had overlooked the call. It wouldn't help to admit that his mind was so full of thoughts of Rebecca that he found it difficult to concentrate on anything else.

'Contact his secretary and ask her to schedule a call for this afternoon around three. I should be finished in Theatre by then. And, please, make sure that letters of confirmation are sent to everyone who has expressed an interest in attending the conference.'

'I have done that already, Dr Valdez. I left them on your desk yesterday for you to sign,' his secretary reminded him primly.

'So you did. Thank you. That will be all for now.'

Felipe managed to hide his dismay until the woman had left, but it worried him that he had forgotten about signing the letters. It just proved how abstracted he had been of late.

He got up and went to the window, thinking about what had happened last night in the pool. He knew that if Josh hadn't woken, he and Rebecca would have ended up in bed together. But would that have been the right thing to do?

He smiled thinly. Right or wrong hadn't entered into it. The moment he'd taken her in his arms he hadn't been able to think of anything apart from making love to her. He ached to hold her even now, and that was why he'd left the villa early that morning before she'd got up. He hadn't trusted himself not to try to carry on where they'd left off, but he had to be sensible until he had spoken to the solicitor in London. Once everything was cleared up, he could do what he wanted most and make her a permanent part of his life.

He could no longer deny that was what he desired more than anything so he didn't try. He had fallen head over heels in love with Rebecca and he wanted her in his life from now till eternity. He hadn't planned on it happening, certainly hadn't expected it to, but it was a fact. He loved her and he sensed that she felt the same about him.

Felipe went back to his desk when the phone rang, feeling his heart lift when his secretary informed him that there was a call for him from London. He found himself smiling as he told her to put it through because it seemed propitious that it should have happened then.

Maybe he would be able to solve the last bit of the puzzle sooner than he'd expected, although it couldn't be soon enough as far as he was concerned. He had a future to plan, a future with Rebecca and Josh.

How very right it felt to know that he would be able to take care of his brother's child.

'You will need to pop up to the administration department and fill in the insurance claim forms. Once that's done you can take Christopher back to the hotel.'

Becky smiled at the little boy. 'You feel a lot better today, don't you, sweetheart?'

Christopher gave her a shy little smile although he didn't say anything. Becky guessed that he'd been a bit scared about having to stay in the hospital on his own, despite the fact that the nurses on duty had lavished attention on him. To be honest, she didn't have much time to spare for his parents after the callous way they'd treated the child, but she tried not to let her feelings show when Michael Thomas drew her aside.

'I thought all this treatment was free because we're in the EU,' he demanded.

'There is a reciprocal arrangement between EU countries for basic health care, but it doesn't cover everything,' she explained politely. 'The administration department will sort it all out if you have a word with them. You'll need to take a copy of your insurance certificate with you. The tour company should have issued you with one before you left England.'

'We didn't buy insurance off the holiday company. It was too expensive.'

Michael was starting to look very uneasy. Becky frowned because she couldn't understand why he had a problem with what should have been a routine matter. 'So you took out a separate policy? That isn't a problem…'

'We didn't buy *any* insurance,' he snapped, glaring at her. 'I couldn't see any point in wasting money when there was no need.'

She bit back a sigh. 'Then I'm afraid that you'll have to pay the bill for any treatment outside of the basics yourself, Mr Thomas. Do you have a credit card with you?' She carried on when he nodded, not giving him the chance to say anything else. 'You will be able to pay the bill with that, then.'

She left him standing there, glaring after her. If it had been anyone else she might have felt a certain sympathy, but not after the way he'd treated his son. She made her way to the nurses' room and poured herself a cup of coffee. It was time for the morning break and there were several other nurses already in there.

She exchanged a few words with them then decided to take her drink onto the terrace. Frankly, she felt as though she needed a bit of breathing space to think about what had happened the night before. Not that it would help her decide what to do, of course. She wanted to tell Felipe the truth but she was afraid. End of story.

She found a sheltered spot on the terrace and sat on a bench to drink her coffee. She'd been surprised when she'd discovered that Felipe had already left the villa by the time she and

Josh had got up. Maybe he'd had an urgent call, although she hadn't heard the telephone ringing. She was just wondering what had happened to him when he appeared, and she laughed.

'I was just thinking about you!'

'Indeed? I wonder what you were plotting this time, Rebecca.'

'Plotting?' she echoed. She looked at him in confusion and felt her heart sink when she saw the expression on his face. He was looking at her as though she were a stranger, someone he barely knew.

She rose unsteadily to her feet, feeling her legs trembling. 'What's happened, Felipe? Why are you looking at me like that after…?' She bit her lip. Did she really want to remind him of last night and the way he'd held her, kissed her, loved her?

Her mind stalled on that word because nobody could look at another person this way and feel love for them.

'After what we did last night? Come, Rebecca, why are you shy to talk about it? You certainly weren't shy at the time as I recall. You were only too willing to let me enjoy your beautiful body, and it didn't happen just the once either. Was the first time to whet my appetite and the second to get me completely under your spell? I really am interested to hear the answer, *querida*.'

'I have no idea what this is all about, but I don't intend to stand here and let you insult me.' She spun on her heel but he was too fast for her. She stopped dead when he stepped in front of her.

'I apologise. I did not come to insult you, Rebecca. I came because I need you to answer a question for me.'

His voice sounded so cold, so distant that it was impossible not to compare it to the way he had spoken to her the night before. Then his voice had been full of warmth and desire, echoing with unspoken promises that made her heart race even now to recall it. It made it doubly difficult to understand what was happening.

'What question? I don't understand…'

'Why did you tell me that you are Josh's mother when it was a lie?'

Felipe saw the colour drain from her face and he felt nothing, neither pleasure nor pain. He felt too numb to feel anything. He heard her drag in a little air and still he felt nothing. All his emotions seemed to have died slowly, agonisingly, when the solicitor had told him the truth at last, that Rebecca wasn't the mother of his brother's child.

'How did you find—?'

He gave a sharp downward thrust of his hand which silenced her. 'It does not matter *how* I found out, it is *what* I found out. Josh is indeed Antonio's son, but he isn't yours. His real mother is Tara Lewis. It is her name on Josh's birth certificate, and before you try to deny it I must warn you that Antonio's solicitor has faxed me a copy of the document.'

He gave a small shrug, knowing that he couldn't bear it if she tried to lie to him again. 'Evidently, he needed to see Josh's birth certificate when he drew up the papers appointing you as the child's guardian. He kept a copy of it for his records.'

'Then there would be no point in me trying to deny it, would there?'

The bleakness in her voice seemed to penetrate the numbing layer that had enveloped him and his hands clenched because he didn't want to feel anything at the moment. All he wanted was to get the facts straight and then decide what he should do.

'Tara Lewis gave birth to Josh and subsequently she and Antonio signed papers appointing you as his guardian,' he said flatly. 'Why? That's the only thing I am interested in at the moment.'

'Because Antonio knew that I would always look after Josh.' Once again she had to struggle to drag in a little air, and another pain pierced the wall around his heart.

'And why would you look after him and not his mother? Surely it was her responsibility, not yours?' He gave a dismissive flick of his hand. 'You were nothing to my brother, were you?'

'No, that's not true! I loved Antonio and he loved me. He knew that he could trust me to look after Josh—'

'And he couldn't trust Tara? Is that what you're claiming?' he shot back. Even though he knew it was wrong to let himself be sidetracked at a time like this, it had hurt unbearably to hear Rebecca claim how much she'd loved his brother.

'No, he couldn't trust her! Tara never wanted Josh. When she found out she was pregnant, she wanted to have an abortion. She went to see Antonio and asked him for the money to pay for it!'

The words were flowing out of her now. Felipe tried to harden his heart, but her anguish was almost more than he could bear. He wanted to gather her into his arms and tell her that it didn't matter what she'd done because he would always love her. But deep inside he knew that it *did* matter. How could he ever trust her when she'd lied to him about something so important?

'Antonio was desperate when he found out what Tara was planning. His affair with her had been over for some time by then, and he'd told me that he'd realised it had been a mistake. But having Tara turn up at that point in his life, telling him that she was pregnant and that she wanted to get rid of the baby, was too much for him to cope with.'

She ran her hands over her face and Felipe realised that she was crying, but he couldn't afford to show her any sympathy. He needed to hear the whole story then put it behind him, only it wouldn't be that simple, of course.

'Why couldn't he cope?' he snapped, trying not to think about the future and the fact that Rebecca could never be a part of it now. Once before he'd been deceived by a woman, but this time it was far worse. He had never loved Teresa as he loved Rebecca. His heart ached because there was no way he could deny it.

'If Antonio was old enough to have got himself into that mess in the first place, he was old enough to deal with it,' he said harshly.

'Maybe he could have done if circumstances had been dif-

ferent,' she said thickly. 'But he'd only just found out that he
had cancer and the doctors had told him that the treatment he
needed would make him sterile. At that stage we were still
hoping that he might be cured, but learning that he would never
be able to father a child came as a huge blow to him.'

Felipe could understand that. It would have been a bitter
blow to him, too, although having children wasn't something
he had thought about for a long time.

He closed his mind when an image of Rebecca—her body
swollen with his child—rushed into his head. It would never
happen now, not after the way she'd lied to him about Josh.
Maybe she'd lied about the rest of it as well, about Antonio
and the money, the way she seemed to feel about him.

It was an effort to focus because that last thought caused
him such pain. How could he believe that Rebecca really felt
anything for him when her whole life might be one huge lie?

'And that's when I came up with the idea to pay Tara to
have the baby.'

'So it was your idea?' He laughed softly, hoping it would
disguise his heartache. 'Why doesn't that surprise me? What
else did you plan, Rebecca? Was it your idea to write Tara out
of her son's life? You say that Tara was paid to have the baby,
but I'm sure you received a lot more than she did. She was the
unfortunate victim in all this, wasn't she? Once she'd had Josh
then you simply dispensed with her.'

'No, you're not listening to me! Tara never wanted Josh.
She had him purely and simply for the money! Why do you
think I needed that twenty thousand pounds?'

She looked him straight in the eye and he could tell that she
was willing him to believe her. 'Tara threatened to go to court
and claim that she'd been coerced into signing over custody of
Josh if I didn't give her more money. She'd had nearly every
penny of Antonio's inheritance and there wasn't anything left.
I tried explaining to her that it could end up with Josh being
taken into care, but she just laughed. She told me that she didn't
care what happened to him so long as she got the money!'

Felipe could hear the ring of truth in her voice, but he was afraid to believe her. He couldn't comprehend that any woman would have handed over her child the way Tara Lewis apparently had.

He realised then that he wasn't capable of thinking rationally at that moment and the matter was too important to make any mistakes. Josh's whole future was at stake. What it all might boil down to was whether or not he was prepared to leave his brother's son in the care of a woman who had lied to him.

'What do you intend to do…about Josh, I mean?'

His heart ached afresh when he heard the fear in her voice, but he couldn't afford to think about Rebecca's feelings. It was Josh who mattered, nobody else. 'I haven't decided yet.'

'I promised Antonio that I would always look after him,' she whispered brokenly. 'No matter how much you might hate me, please, don't take Josh away from me, Felipe. I…I don't think I could bear it if I had to give him up.'

'Maybe you should have thought about that sooner,' he said bitterly. He shook his head when she went to speak. 'No. I need time to think about this. My only concern from now on has to be Josh. I have to do the right thing for him.'

'Even if that means applying for custody of him?'

'If that is what I decide will be best for him in the long term, then yes, although obviously his real mother's wishes must also be taken into account.'

'Tara doesn't care what happens to him. I've told you that!' she exclaimed. 'Please, please, don't make the mistake of thinking that Josh might be better off with her.'

'You have told me a lot of things, Rebecca. Some may have been true, others obviously weren't.' His tone was uncompromising and he saw her flinch.

'I wanted to tell you the truth, Felipe. Really I did…'

'It doesn't matter now.' Suddenly, he knew that he couldn't bear to hear any more. It wouldn't help to know how much she was hurting and that he was responsible for it. 'The only thing that concerns me now is Josh.'

He turned and walked away. Rebecca was still standing where he'd left her when he reached the end of the terrace and

looked back. He let his eyes rest on her for one last moment
then carried on, and it felt as though a door had closed and
he'd been plunged into darkness.

There was no future to look forward to now. Oh, he would
do his utmost for his brother's child. If he did apply for custody
of Josh and was successful he would love and care for him to
the very best of his ability, but there would be no pleasure in
it because Rebecca wouldn't be there with him, helping him,
loving him, bringing light and warmth into his life.

How empty his world was going to be without her.

Becky stared after Felipe, wishing with her whole heart that
she could make her body obey her. She wanted to run after
him and make him believe that she'd wanted to tell him the
truth, but she couldn't move. All the strength seemed to have
drained from her limbs so that she could only stand and watch
him walking away from her. And she knew in that moment
that it really was the end, the end of her dreams and maybe
the end of her role in Josh's life as well.

Tears clogged her throat but her eyes were dry. The grief
she felt ran too deep to find an outlet in tears. Somehow she
made herself walk back into the hospital and it was as though
she were suddenly a stranger in the familiar environment.
Everything was the same as it always had been: the quiet bustle
of the ward; the murmur of voices; the smell of antiseptic that
hung in the air. The world was carrying on as normal and it
was just for her that life had come to a halt. From this point
on she had no future to look forward to.

She managed to get through the morning, but it felt as
though she were functioning on autopilot. She was pro-
grammed to react to various situations and she did. She spoke
to Diane and Tim Ryan, comforted parents whose little girl had
broken her arm, gave out drugs and checked obs, and afterwards she couldn't recall what she'd done. It scared her to
realise that because it was too risky for the patients.

She went for lunch, wondering what she should do. She
would have to leave, of course, because she couldn't stay at

the clinic now and certainly couldn't continue living in Felipe's house. She would have to go back to England, take Josh with her, see if she could hide him away so that Felipe couldn't find him...

'Becky!'

She jumped when someone called her name. Turning, she stared in bewilderment at the red-haired man who was hurrying towards her. For a moment she had no idea who he was before she realised it was Simon Montague.

'What are you doing here?' she asked faintly.

'I've come to see my cousin—Richard Jeffries. Remember, the chap who broke his neck diving into a swimming pool?' Simon stared at her when she didn't answer. 'Richie said that he'd met you, Becky. You must remember him?'

'I...um...yes, of course. I...I had no idea he was your cousin, though.' She tried to smile but her mouth wouldn't seem to work and she saw Simon look at her in concern.

'Are you OK? I didn't mean to give you a shock, really I didn't.' He looked momentarily uncomfortable. 'I may as well come clean and admit that I knew you were working here. As soon as I heard that Richie was in the Clinica Valdez I made the connection. But I didn't mean to...well, upset you.'

'You haven't,' she said quickly. 'It's not you, Simon. I've just had a bad day....' She bit her lip when she felt a sob rise to her throat.

Simon shot a look along the busy corridor then quickly steered her into an alcove. 'Tell me what's happened. And before you try to deny it, I can tell there's something wrong.' His pleasant face tightened all of a sudden. 'Has Valdez done something to upset you?'

'It's all very complicated,' she began, not wanting to involve him in her affairs.

Simon shook his head impatiently. 'No, you're not going to get away that easily. I want to know what's wrong, Becky. I thought we were friends and I want to help you any way I can.'

Her eyes filled with tears when she heard the concern in his voice. 'Oh, Simon, it's such a mess. I never meant this to happen. All I ever wanted to do was help Antonio and look after Josh.'

All of a sudden the whole miserable story came pouring out. To give Simon his due, he didn't interrupt her even though she could see how shocked he was by what he heard. She wiped her eyes with the handkerchief he gave her and looked miserably up at him.

'I've made a real mess of everything, haven't I?'

'No, you haven't. I can't think of anyone who would have done what you've done.'

It was such a relief to hear him say that. Tears welled from her eyes again. She didn't protest when Simon put his arms around her and hugged her. He gave a deep sigh then slowly loosened his hold on her.

'Now we need to decide what you must do. Obviously you can't stay here so you'll have to go back to England.'

'I know, but I don't have any money for the fare. And even if I do go back, I've nowhere to live, no job…nothing.'

'That isn't a problem. I'll pay your fare and you and Josh can stay with me while you find somewhere to live. I'll be staying in Mallorca for a few days to be with Richie so I'll give you the key to my flat. As for a job, well, they'll take you back at St Leonard's like a shot. They've not found anyone to replace you, so we've been making do with agency nurses when we can get them.'

'Oh, but I couldn't,' she protested. 'I don't mean the job, but I couldn't let you pay my air fare. And as for putting us up…'

'Becky, it isn't a problem! Really.' He took hold of her hands and squeezed them. 'I want to help you but, please, don't worry that you might be giving me the wrong idea.' He shrugged. 'I realise that we can be nothing more than friends, but that's OK.'

'I don't know what to say, Simon. It's so good of you…'

She tailed off when she caught sight of Felipe coming along the corridor. Her heart felt as though it was being slowly squeezed to pulp when she saw the coldness on his face as he spotted her and Simon.

He passed them without saying a word and his very silence was enough to tell her how pointless it would be to go after him. He would never believe that she'd wanted so desperately to tell him the truth.

She took a deep breath but it did nothing to ease the agony she felt. 'Thank you, Simon. I really appreciate this.'

'You don't have to thank me, Becky. I'm happy to help.' Simon stared after Felipe and for a moment she thought he was going to say something before he thought better of it.

'I'll sort out a plane ticket for you. What time will you be ready to leave? I might be able to get you a seat on a flight today if that's not too soon.'

'No,' she said hollowly. 'The sooner I leave here the better it will be for everyone concerned.'

Simon hurried off to make the arrangements while Becky collected Josh from the crèche and took him back to the villa. She packed only the things she had brought with her and left behind all the beautiful toys and clothes that Felipe had provided for him. They weren't hers to take and she wouldn't give him the chance to accuse her of stealing from him.

Tears slid down her cheeks and she dashed them away, but more kept on coming. She picked Josh up and held him close, drawing comfort from the feel of his sturdy little body in her arms.

How long she would be able to keep him was another matter, of course. But whatever happened, she would make sure that he was never handed over to Tara. She didn't really believe that Tara would want him, but there was always a chance that Tara might change her mind if she could see any financial benefit in having Josh.

If it came to a court case she would tell the judge the whole story, present him with all the evidence to back it up and make sure that Josh was placed in Felipe's care. No matter how much Felipe hated her, he would do his best for Josh.

He would give his brother's child all the love that he could never give her.

Felipe made his way to Theatre and scrubbed up. It was a fairly routine operation, the removal of a gallstone laparoscopically—minimally invasive surgery performed through a tiny incision using a laparoscope. It was an operation which he'd performed dozens of times before so he wasn't anticipating any problems, yet he found that his hands were shaking when he turned off the taps.

He made himself breathe deeply, but the tremor didn't stop. He could feel his muscles bunching and flickering, feel the ligaments and nerves jerking beneath his skin, and realised that he was in no fit state to carry out even the simplest procedure if he didn't manage to control himself. But seeing Rebecca standing there in another man's arms had already tested his self-control to its limit.

He swore softly, fluently, and Domingo, who was standing beside him at the sink, shot him a worried look. 'Are you all right, Dr Valdez?'

'Yes!' he snapped, holding out his hands for the sterile towel Theatre Sister had ready for him. It fell from his grasp and he stared at it lying there on the floor while images played in front of his eyes, images of Rebecca with that man's arms around her, her slender body pressed against his, her face tilted up as she waited for him to kiss her...

Felipe swung round, ignoring the startled looks that Domingo and the nurse exchanged. 'I am unable to continue with this operation. Have Dr Ramirez paged and ask her to take over from me.'

He didn't wait to hear what Domingo said as he strode from the room. Tossing his paper hat into the waste basket, he left Theatre and made his way to the stairs. He didn't stop to change from his scrub suit into his clothes and he saw several members of staff stare at him in astonishment as he passed them.

He had made it a strict rule that everyone must be properly

dressed at all times, but he didn't give a damn about appearances at that moment. He didn't give a damn about anything
except finding Rebecca and making her explain what she'd
been doing with that man, Montague, and why he had been in
the clinic. Was this another one of her schemes, another way
to make use of every man she came into contact with?

Anger ripped through him and the fact that it was mixed
with a burning jealousy he hadn't believed himself capable of
just made him feel worse. He didn't want to be jealous about
a woman who had lied to him, but he couldn't stop himself.

He left the hospital and made his way to the villa, knowing
instinctively that she would be there. He only hoped that
Montague wasn't with her because he wouldn't be responsible
for his actions if he found the man in his house.

Rebecca was in the hall and she jumped when he flung open
the door. He just had a moment to take in her tear-stained face
before he caught sight of the cases at her feet. His eyes
skimmed over the battered suitcase and the cheap shoulder-bag
stuffed with Josh's nappies and bottles, while a piercing pain
ran through his heart as he realised that she was leaving. It
took every scrap of strength he possessed to open his mouth
and speak.

'Where are you going?'

'Back to London.'

Her voice wobbled and he saw her bite her lip. His hands
clenched when he saw that she'd bitten it so hard that she'd
drawn blood. He ached to take her in his arms and kiss it better,
let his lips heal that tiny wound, but he couldn't do that. He
couldn't let himself forget what she had done.

'And what if I refuse to let you leave?' he said hoarsely
instead.

'You can't stop me, Felipe.' Her head came up and despite
the tears on her cheeks and the pain in her eyes there was a
quiet dignity about her that shamed him. 'I'm Josh's legal
guardian and until the courts decide differently I'm free to take
him back to England, or anywhere else I choose. It goes with-

out saying that you have no hold over me now that I've terminated my contract at the clinic.'

'You know that I'll probably sue for custody of the boy?' he shot back, stung by that last comment. He had no hold over her because she didn't care about him. She didn't love him; his feelings didn't matter; it had all been an act.

'Yes. And if I can't have Josh, I hope you win, Felipe. In fact, you have my word that I shall do everything in my power to make sure that you get custody of him.' She brushed a gentle kiss over the top of the baby's head then looked him straight in the eye.

'I won't run away with Josh. I won't try to hide him. I did think about it but I realise that it would be the wrong thing to do. However, I shall do everything in my power to ensure that Tara never gets him back.'

She gave a husky laugh and he felt his eyes burn with sudden tears when he heard the sadness it held, the pain. 'I know that you will love and care for Antonio's precious son every bit as much as I would have done. It will be some consolation.'

Felipe didn't know what to say. He'd never dreamt that she would want to entrust Josh into his care if the child couldn't stay with her.

Once again his emotions shifted, swirling like sand in a desert storm. Had he been wrong? Should he have let her explain why she hadn't told him the truth about Josh? Did it *really* need explaining or could he work it out for himself? Had Rebecca not told him purely and simply because she'd been afraid of losing the baby?

Questions raced through his mind and he jumped when she suddenly bent and picked up her case.

'The taxi's arrived. I'll have to go.' He heard her swallow, heard the thickness of her voice as she added, 'Don't hate me too much, Felipe. I only did what I thought was right for Josh.'

She went to the door, murmuring her thanks when he opened it for her, and it was the fact that she could thank him after everything he'd said to her that moved him unbearably.

He watched her climb into the cab, saw how carefully she

settled Josh on her lap, how tenderly she held the little boy in her arms, and saw nothing else. Tears filled his eyes and he couldn't see the taxi as it drove away. Maybe that was a good thing. Maybe it would stop his heart breaking if he didn't have to watch her leaving.

Maybe.

CHAPTER TWELVE

'IT's great to have you back! At least we'll have someone here who knows what she's doing!'

Becky laughed. It was her first day back at St Leonard's and the first person she'd met on her arrival had been Karen. As they travelled up to the IC unit together in the lift, she made a determined effort to be cheerful.

Simon had assured her that nobody knew the real reason why she'd come back to England and she knew that she could trust him. He had been a wonderful support, letting her and Josh stay at his flat then helping her find a place of her own and lending her the money for the deposit.

She'd managed to find a tiny one bedroom flat close to where she'd lived before, so Josh had gone back to the same child-minder. He had settled in straight away and it was a relief to know that he was happy.

As Simon had predicted, the hospital had been only too eager to take her back. They had even waived the usual interview and had simply asked her when she could start. Now all she had to do was convince everyone that she'd returned to London because she'd been homesick and she could start putting her life back together, or as together as it was possible to be in the circumstances.

'I'm sure it can't have been that bad,' she said, trying not to think about what might happen in the coming weeks. Felipe hadn't made any attempt to contact her even though she had written to tell him her new address. However, she intended to keep her word and do everything in her power to help him gain custody of Josh if it came to a court case.

'Simon told me that you'd had agency nurses covering my post.'

'If and when they could find any.' Karen sighed as the lift came to a stop. 'It's easier finding gold in the Thames than it is to find qualified IC nurses, especially paediatric ones. I can't count the number of double shifts I've worked since you left.'

'Really? I suppose that explains why the powers that be welcomed me back with open arms,' she suggested wryly.

'That, plus the fact that you're one of the best IC nurses we've ever had in the unit,' Karen said generously. 'I was really sorry that it didn't work out for you in Mallorca, but their loss is our gain. I only hope that Josh's uncle didn't give you too hard a time.'

'What do you mean?' she asked, her heart sinking. Had something leaked out after all about what had gone on?

'Well, I don't suppose he was very pleased about you leaving after he'd made all the arrangements for you to move over there,' Karen replied, leading the way along the corridor. 'He didn't strike me as the sort of man who would take kindly to having his plans disrupted.'

'No, he isn't,' Becky agreed hollowly. She tried not to think about Felipe too often, but it wasn't easy to shut him out. Now, she sighed as an image of his handsome face swam before her eyes.

She missed him so much! Every day that passed just made it harder to cope. If only he'd let her explain why she hadn't told him the truth about Josh. If she could believe that he didn't hate her, it would help to ease the pain just a little.

'You OK? I didn't say something I shouldn't, did I?' Karen grimaced when she looked blankly at her. 'Simon has been rather evasive whenever I've asked about you. I did wonder if there was more to your return than he told us.'

'Hardly!' Becky summoned a smile, not wanting Karen to start asking any awkward questions. 'I got homesick for good old London. End of story. Anyway, what's been going on here? What happened at the inquest into Rosie Stokes's death?' she asked, briskly changing the subject.

'Oh, it was all St Ada's fault, as we knew it was. Turned out that they'd run out of blood and borrowed some from St

Leonard's until their own supplies arrived. That accounted for the discrepancy in the bar-code.'

Karen was successfully distracted and Becky breathed a sigh of relief as she followed her into the staffroom. 'And how about the mix-up with the blood groups?'

'St Ada's again. They only went and left their most junior trainee to change poor little Rosie's drip.' Karen's face mirrored her disgust. 'She mixed up the blood with some intended for another patient and nobody double-checked. Fortunately, another nurse realised there had been a mistake, so the other poor soul didn't get the wrong transfusion. But nobody followed it up to see what had gone wrong.'

'Incredible!' Becky exclaimed. 'I don't know why people can't just follow the rules. Someone should have checked the trainee's work. Imagine how awful it would have been if Debbie had been blamed for what happened.'

'She was completely exonerated before the inquiry. Danny Epstein—remember him, the boy with endocarditis?' Karen carried on when she nodded. 'Well, Danny's mum saw Debbie settling Rosie in and was able to testify that she hadn't changed the transfusion. She's a lawyer, as it happens, so she was very precise about what she said.'

'How wonderful! I was afraid it would be the last straw and Debbie would ask for a transfer,' she admitted.

Karen laughed. 'Funnily enough, it's done just the opposite. She's far more confident than she used to be. Odd how adversity sometimes brings out the best in folk, isn't it?'

Becky nodded, but her heart felt heavy all of a sudden. Would it bring out the best in her if Felipe took her to court to claim custody of Josh? How would she cope if she didn't have Josh to give meaning to her life? She could never have Felipe now, of course, and the thought of how empty her life might be in the future was almost more than she could bear.

Felipe had taken some time off work because he was more of a hindrance than a help. He knew that his colleagues were starting to wonder what was wrong with him, but he didn't care. Where once the affairs of the Clinica Valdez had been his sole reason for getting up of a morning, he now found himself unable to take any interest in what was going on there.

He appointed one of his senior colleagues as director in his absence and left it at that. If...and it was a very big *if* at this stage...he managed to get his life back on track, he would resume his duties. Maybe one day the clinic would take centre stage in his life again, but at the moment it was Rebecca who had claimed that role.

He missed her so much! Missed the sound of her laughter, the comfort of her silence. He missed just knowing that she was there in the villa. He missed her more than he'd believed it possible to miss another human being, and it was slowly but surely driving him to the edge of despair.

He knew that he would have to do something to resolve the situation before he drove himself completely crazy, but it wasn't until he heard a bulletin on the midday news three weeks after Rebecca had returned to London that he was shocked into action.

He sat on the edge of his chair as the reporter told of a fire which had swept through St Leonard's Hospital in London. There were pictures of the burning building, along with scenes of staff ferrying patients outside. It was hard to take it all in, especially when the reporter mentioned that several members of the hospital's staff had been injured in the blaze.

Was Rebecca one of them? Was she even now lying in another hospital's bed, in pain, maybe dying?

He felt sick at the thought of losing her. He couldn't bear it if he had to live out the rest of his days without the comfort of knowing that she was alive and well somewhere in the world. All of a sudden, it was that thought which drove the confusion from his head.

Yes, she had lied to him about being Josh's mother, but she had done it purely out of fear for the child. She had wanted to protect Josh, make sure that no harm came to him.

Everything she'd done, from promising Antonio to always take care of his son to visiting the clinic that day to ask him for money, had been done for Josh. She had put the child's welfare before her own, been prepared to suffer any kind of hardship so long as the child was happy. Even the fact that she'd promised to support *him* if he sued for custody had been typical of her commitment to the boy. Right from the beginning, Rebecca had put Josh's needs before her own.

It was a huge relief to have realised the truth at last, but terrifying that he might have arrived at it too late. If Rebecca had been gravely injured, he might never have the chance to beg her forgiveness and tell her how much he loved her.

He phoned the airport and tried to book a seat to London, barely able to curb his impatience when he was told there weren't any available that day. When the ticket agent suggested making a detour via Madrid he immediately agreed, not caring how long it took him or how many changes he would need to make. So long as he got to London and could be with Rebecca, that was all that mattered.

He could only pray that she was unharmed.

The fire had started in the laundry and had swept through two floors of the hospital before it had been brought under control. The accident and emergency department had been gutted as well as Women's Surgical. It had been a terrifying ordeal for everyone concerned.

The fact that all the patients had needed to be evacuated had put everyone under a great deal of pressure. Wheeling seriously injured people through the billowing clouds of smoke had been a nightmare. Several of the nursing staff had been overcome by fumes and one of the A and E doctors had been seriously injured. A section of the ceiling had fallen on him when he'd gone back to rescue an old lady who'd been trapped in the toilets. He'd been transferred to a specialist spinal unit and the prognosis wasn't good.

The children in the IC unit were transferred to St Ada's, which was rather ironic after recent events. Becky and the rest of the team from the unit did their best to make the transfer as smooth as possible, but it was a worrying time for them all.

Moving gravely injured children across London was an ordeal, and she was glad when it was time to go off duty. Sister Reece had told them to report to St Ada's the following day, although whether they would continue to run the department from there was still being discussed.

Becky was exhausted by the time she collected Josh from the childminder. She took him home and put him in his play-pen while she changed out of her smoke-tainted clothes. She filled the bath and then to Josh's delight got in it with him, washing them both then playing a game of splash in which she came off worst.

It reminded her poignantly of the time Felipe had helped her bath Josh and had told her about his experiences with the doll, Esmeralda. She could recall the surprise in his eyes when he'd admitted that he'd told nobody else the story.

All of a sudden she was crying. Maybe it was the stress of the past few weeks, combined with the events of that day, but she couldn't seem to stop the tears from pouring down her cheeks. Josh looked at her uncertainly, his small face pucker-ing, and it was that which helped her compose herself. The last thing she wanted was Josh being upset.

'It's OK, darling. Mummy's fine,' she told him, but he still looked unsure.

She climbed out of the bath and put on her old towelling robe then lifted him out and dried him, singing his favourite nursery rhymes to distract him. He looked a little happier by the time she went to fetch his bedtime milk and soon settled down once he'd drunk it. He was drifting off to sleep when she heard the doorbell ringing. She hurried to answer it, not wanting it to wake him.

Becky slipped the chain on the door because she wasn't sure who it would be. Simon had been her only visitor so far, so maybe he'd come to update her about what was happening. She knew that there were concerns about the IC unit remaining at St Ada's so they might have decided to relocate it some-where else.

All that was whizzing through her head as she opened the

door so the last thing she'd expected was to find Felipe standing outside. Just for a moment she stared at him with her heart
in her eyes before she dragged her gaze away.

'What do you want?' she asked hoarsely.

'To see if you were all right. I heard the report on the news
about the fire. It said there were people injured…nursing
staff…'

She heard him take a deep breath, heard the raw note of fear
in his voice when he continued, and it was that which made
her heart start to thunder inside her. To hear him sounding so
scared shook her to the depths of her being because she didn't
understand what it meant.

'I was worried about you, Rebecca. I had to come.'

Felipe held his breath, praying that she would believe him.
Knowing that she was safe was such a relief.

He had been so scared on the flight from Madrid, terrified
of what he might find when he arrived. He'd taken a taxi from
Heathrow, his mind whirling this way and that yet always coming back to the thought of what he would do if Rebecca had
been killed in the fire. He couldn't even contemplate living out
the rest of his life without her…

'Worried about me? You really expect me to believe that?'

He flinched when she gave a bitter little laugh, felt his stomach roil with sickness when he saw the disbelief in her eyes.
He could barely contain his pain when he realised that he was
responsible for it.

'Yes. I know you must find it hard to believe, Rebecca, and
I understand why you feel that way. I behaved abominably. All
I can do now is apologise and hope that you will forgive me.'

'What is the point?' she said in a tone that made him ache
because it held so much anguish. 'You hate me because I didn't
tell you the truth about not being Josh's real mother. Nothing
is going to change that fact, is it?'

'I don't hate you, Rebecca. I never could!' He felt his heart
swell with tenderness when he saw the sudden uncertainty in
her eyes. He sensed that she desperately wanted to believe him

and it was that which suddenly made it easy to tell her the truth.

'I love you, Rebecca. I love you with my whole heart and if you feel anything at all for me, please, let me come in. We can work this out if it's what we both want, I promise you.'

'You love me?' She closed her eyes and he saw the lines of strain that were etched on her beautiful face. 'If this is a trick, Felipe…'

'*Dios!* Do you think I would lie about such a thing?' he demanded. 'I love you. My life is empty without you. I cannot work, cannot sleep, cannot even think! That is why I had to come and see if you were all right. I…I couldn't go on if anything had happened to you.'

His voice broke and he turned away, unable to stand there while she refused to believe him. Maybe he deserved to be treated like this after everything he'd done, but it hurt. It hurt so much!

'Wait!'

He paused, one hand gripping the banister when he heard her call out to him. He couldn't turn, couldn't speak, couldn't do anything except wait and, maybe, hope.

'Don't go. Please. Not yet.'

He heard her footsteps coming along the landing, heard them stop, and still he couldn't move. He seemed to be frozen, waiting for her to say or do something, hoping—praying—that it would be what he wanted so much.

'Did you mean it, Felipe? Do…do you really love me?'

The hope in her voice was the catalyst that unlocked his mind and body, and he turned towards her. He knew that she could see the truth in his eyes even before he answered her question.

'Yes, Rebecca. I meant it. I love you. Really.'

'Oh, I never dreamt…never thought…'

Suddenly she was laughing and crying at the same time but more importantly she was walking towards him. Felipe opened his arms and as she stepped into them he knew he would never let her go again.

She tipped back her head and he could see the love in her eyes as he heard her say the words, 'I love you, Felipe.'

He kissed her then, gently, tenderly, and the moment he felt her lips under his he was filled with certainty. Rebecca loved him. He loved her. They were two constants upon which they could build their future, no matter what happened.

Becky wasn't sure how long they stood there with their arms wrapped around one another. It was only when she heard the front door slam and footsteps coming up the stairs that she realised how public a place they had chosen to declare their love for each other. She stepped out of Felipe's arms, smiling tenderly when she saw the bemusement on his face.

'I think we should continue this in my flat, don't you?'

He blinked and she saw him look around uncertainly before a slow smile curved his mouth. '*Sí, querida.* We are in danger of shocking your neighbours, I fear.'

She laughed softly as she led the way into the flat and closed the door. Felipe reached for her again and kissed her hungrily, and she shuddered as she felt desire starting to burn inside her. It was an effort to speak when he raised his head.

'It's a good job we did move. We could have caused a riot out there on the stairs.'

Felipe laughed, taking her hand and pulling her back into his arms for one last kiss before he reluctantly let her go. 'We shall confine our love-making to the privacy of your home from now on, my darling. But first there are things we need to talk about. *Sí?*'

'You mean Josh and Tara and everything?' She sighed when he nodded. 'You're right, of course. It's just that I'm—'

'Afraid that I will not understand?' He looked deep into her eyes and she saw the assurance his held. 'I shall, Rebecca. Just tell me what happened, right from the beginning. We need to put this behind us once and for all.'

She smiled because she knew that he meant it. 'Let's go into the sitting-room, or what passes for a sitting-room. I'm afraid it's rather cramped.'

She led the way, smiling ruefully when she saw the expression on his face. 'Not the height of luxury but it's served its purpose for the past few weeks.'

'I hate to think of you and Josh having to live here.' He cast an expressive glance around the dingy room then made an obvious effort to ignore it as he sat beside her on the lumpy sofa. Lifting her hand, he pressed a kiss to her palm then closed her fingers over the tingling little spot as though he wanted her to feel the evidence of his love while she related her tale. And in an odd sort of way it helped.

'You said to start from the beginning so I shall. I met Antonio by chance one day when we were both using the local launderette.' She smiled. 'He'd put all his washing in together and one of his shirts had been stained by dye from a T-shirt. I offered to take it home and see if I could get the stains out of it for him.'

Felipe laughed. 'Antonio must have found it difficult doing things for himself because Maria had always taken care of us.'

'He did at first, but he soon learned,' she assured him. 'After that we started going out together. I think we were both rather lonely, to be honest. Antonio had recently split with Tara and my mother had died a few months earlier. My father died when I was a toddler so it was just Mum and me, and we were very close.'

'I wish I could have been there for you,' he said huskily and she smiled at him because it was such a lovely thought.

'I wish you had, too. Anyway, Antonio told me about his relationship with Tara not long after we started going out together. He said that he regretted getting involved with her and I believed him.' She sighed softly. 'He never made any secret of the fact that he loved me.'

'And you loved him, too, didn't you, Rebecca?'

She heard the pain in his voice and knew at once what had caused it. She framed his face between his hands and looked deep into his eyes. 'Yes, I loved Antonio, but not the way I love you. He was the sweetest, gentlest man I've ever known.'

Felipe turned his head so that he could brush her palm with a kiss, and she heard the tears that had thickened his voice.

'Thank you for being there when he needed you, Rebecca. Thank you for caring about him enough to make him feel loved. It helps to know that he had you with him when he died.'

Her own eyes filled with tears as she drew him into her arms and held him. 'I only ever wanted to help him, Felipe. Everything I did was for him and for Josh.'

'I know that. I really do.' He kissed her quickly on the lips then wiped away her tears and smiled at her. 'So, please, tell me what happened.'

'Tara's announcement that she was pregnant came like a bolt from the blue. Antonio knew what she was like, that she was only really interested in money and having a good time. Even though he regretted having got involved with her, he couldn't bear the thought that she was going to abort his child, especially when he might never be able to have any children in the future.'

'And that was when you came up with the idea of paying her to have the baby?' he suggested gently.

'Yes. It probably sounds crazy to you, but Antonio was so distraught I had to do something to help him. Finding out that he had cancer was such a devastating blow, especially when it turned out to be such an aggressive form.'

'Fibrosarcoma is one of the most difficult cancers to treat, especially if it has spread throughout the body,' he observed sadly.

'Which was what had happened in Antonio's case. I tried to give him all the support I could, but there was very little I could do.'

'You were there for him, Rebecca. That was the most important thing of all.'

She sighed when she heard the pain in his voice. 'You're wishing that he'd told you, aren't you? He did think about it. We spoke about you a lot, in fact. Even though you two had argued, he loved you very much, Felipe. He just felt that he had to face what happened on his own and make his own decisions. He was afraid that you might not let him and that the

time might come when he wouldn't have the strength to fight
you.'

'And he was right. I would have tried to persuade him to
carry on with the treatment, but now I can see that would have
been the wrong thing to do.'

His voice echoed with regret and she squeezed his hand.
'You loved him and Antonio knew that. Never forget that.' She
carried on when he nodded, knowing that it would be easier if
she stuck to the facts. 'Paying Tara to have the baby seemed
like the best thing to do.'

'And she agreed? The promise of money was enough to
make her decide whether her child should live or die?'

'Yes, I'm afraid it was. All Tara was interested in was the
money, and she made sure that she got as much as possible
out of Antonio. She demanded fifty thousand pounds immediately with another five thousand each month for the duration
of her pregnancy to cover her living expenses.'

She heard him curse under his breath and sighed. 'There
were also credit-card bills and payments on a car she'd bought.
Then there was the money she asked Antonio for to buy baby
clothes, only she never spent it on Josh.'

'And that's why you had to buy everything second-hand?'
He stood up and paced the room, as though he couldn't bear
to remain still while he listened to what she had to say.

'Yes. I had a little money left in my savings account so I
used that. I'd given up my agency job to look after Antonio
and I hadn't been earning for a while so it wasn't very much,
I'm afraid.'

'And what about the money Antonio left you in his will?'
he asked gently as he sat down again.

'That was for Tara, her final payment for having Josh—
another fifty thousand pounds.' She shrugged. 'He didn't trust
Tara not to get rid of the baby so the agreement was that I
would pay her the money after the child was born. Of course,
he hoped to leave enough money for me to take care of Josh,
but Tara had drained his account almost dry. Antonio never

fully realised how much of it he'd handed over to her, and I never told him because it would have upset him too much.'

'*Dios!* I find it hard to believe that any woman could be so...so callous. Did she not change her mind after the child was born?' he demanded.

'On the contrary. She couldn't wait to get rid of Josh and get her hands on the final payment due to her. She handed him over outside the hospital and I never saw her again until she turned up at my flat, demanding another twenty thousand pounds. I was so scared!'

She started shaking and she heard Felipe bite out something harsh in Spanish as he drew her into his arms and held her tightly. 'Shh, *querida*. There is no need to be afraid. Tara will never get her hands on our precious child. I swear on my life that I shall not allow that to happen!'

'You don't know how wonderful it is to hear you say that.' Becky lifted her face and kissed him lightly on the mouth, let the kiss deepen when he immediately responded. This time the tremor that passed through her owed itself to something other than fear, and she smiled shakily.

'I love you so much, Felipe. Have I told you that?'

'Yes, but I can stand hearing it as many times as you care to repeat it.' His eyes were full of warmth and tenderness, his lips full of love, and every last tiny bit of fear melted away. Felipe would always take care of her and Josh.

He let her go with marked reluctance. 'I love you, Rebecca. I only wish that you hadn't had to suffer the way you have. I only wish that Antonio had told me what was happening because I would have understood.'

She sighed softly when she heard the regret in his voice. 'I'm sure he knew that, but he didn't want your life being disrupted by having to raise his child. You were busy with the opening of the clinic and he said something about you having had to give up such a lot for his sake already.'

Felipe sighed. 'He must have meant when I broke off my engagement to Teresa. He was always a sensitive child and he blamed himself, although there was no need. Teresa was having an affair with a friend of mine and that is why we ended our engagement. She wanted a man who would dance attendance on her and I wasn't prepared to do that when I had my life mapped out.'

'You mean setting up the Clinica Valdez?' she guessed.

'Yes. I gave up everything to achieve my dream. Now I realise that I missed out on so much by doing so.'

'You mean Teresa?' It was hard to keep the ache out of her voice and he laughed in delight.

'No, I do not mean Teresa! My pride was hurt when I found out what had been going on, but my heart certainly wasn't broken. I meant that I had missed out on enjoying things other than my work. Isn't there a saying the Americans use about waking up and smelling the coffee? Well, that's what I never did.'

It was so ridiculous that she laughed. 'I can easily make you some coffee, Felipe, if that's what you want!'

'Wretched woman! How dare you tease a man who has been in such torment?'

'Have you? Been in torment, I mean?' she said huskily.

Felipe smiled at her, seeing the love in her eyes. His heart seemed to overflow because he knew it was all for him.

'Yes, my darling. I have been in the worst kind of torment possible because I had lost the one thing that mattered most to me—you.'

'You haven't lost me. I'm here now and I intend to stay right by your side.' She leant forward and there was a world of promise in the kiss she gave him. 'I love you, Felipe.'

'I love you, too.' He chuckled wryly. 'I was *so* jealous when I saw you with Montague at the clinic that day. I have never wanted to hit anyone, but I wanted to hit him!'

'Poor Simon. He's been a good friend and I hope that you two will try to get on.'

He glowered at the idea then sighed when she gave him a stern look. 'Very well, I shall try. But I am more concerned about what will happen to us—you, me and Josh.'

'I am still afraid that Tara might do as she threatened and

go to court out of spite,' she admitted worriedly. 'I'm sure she will try to demand more money at some point, and she won't be pleased if we refuse to pay her.'

'I do not believe that any judge would find in her favour once you had told them the truth, Rebecca. However, we need to bring this to a proper conclusion. I do not want you spending your life worrying what might happen.'

He kissed her quickly, his tongue teasing so tantalisingly around her lips that she groaned. He knew his expression was more than a little smug when he drew back, but he couldn't help it. Rebecca loved him. He felt ten feet tall and as though he could climb mountains. And nothing was going to spoil their happiness from now on.

'I shall sort everything out. Trust me. And now do you think we can steal a few minutes for ourselves? I have come a long way to see you, Rebecca, and it seems a shame to waste this visit by talking all the time.'

She laughed softly, her grey eyes sparkling as she looked at him. 'I thought talking was good for the soul, Dr Valdez?'

'Is it?' He kissed her once on the lips, then a second time on the jaw, feeling the tremor that ran through her as his mouth moved to her throat and began its descent.

'Oh, yes. Very good…'

He heard her breath catch as his mouth slid over her collarbone and carried on with its journey. All she had on was a towelling robe and the V-neckline was the perfect spot to aim for.

A shudder ran through him when he felt the soft swell of small breasts beneath his lips as they travelled towards their goal. Her skin was so warm and smooth, the scent of soap making his body hum with anticipation. He reached the base of the V and planted a kiss there, smiling when he felt her shiver.

'So, do I take it that you still prefer to talk, Rebecca?' he asked, his lips brushing against her skin.

'I suppose it all depends what other choice there is,' she said huskily, and he had to bite back a laugh of delight when he realised how much effort it had cost her to force out the sentence.

'Then perhaps I should help you make up your mind by showing you what is on offer,' he suggested with a wickedly sexy laugh.

He drew the folds of her robe apart and turned so that he could kiss first one nipple and then the other, hearing the moan that came from her lips. It was such a heady experience that he did it all over again then realised that it was he who was moaning this time.

He stood up and lifted her into his arms, smiling down at her with eyes full of love. 'Talking might be good for the soul, Rebecca, but it does very little to ease the ache in one's body, I fear.'

'Then maybe it's time we did something about that.' She wound her arms around his neck, pulled his head down so that she could kiss him lightly on the mouth then smiled. 'Do you think it might help if we made love? It's only a suggestion, of course. Feel free to disagree if you wish.'

'Oh, I think it might help quite a lot.' He returned her kiss then drew back and looked at her. And he knew that he had never meant anything more in his whole life as he continued, 'I love you, Rebecca. I shall spend my life making you happy if you will let me.'

'Good. Although for a man who isn't keen on words, you do seem to spend an awful lot of time talking,' she said pertly, smiling at him.

'Don't worry, *querida*. I do not intend to say anything else for a long time to come!'

He quickly carried her into the bedroom and laid her down on the bed. Josh was fast asleep in his cot and didn't stir. Felipe undid the belt of her robe and pushed it off her shoulders.

Her body was smooth and firm in the glow from the nightlight, her skin gleaming like mother-of-pearl. He was almost afraid to touch her because she looked so fragile, so delicate. But then she reached up to him and her arms were surprisingly strong as she pulled him down to her and held him tightly against her heart.

'Love me, Felipe,' she whispered. 'Just love me.'

'I shall. Always.'

It was the easiest promise he had ever made, and one which he would never break. He would love Rebecca from now until eternity…

Six months later…

'Is that from the solicitor?'

Felipe heard the anxiety in Rebecca's voice as she came into the study where he'd been opening the day's post. He turned and smiled at her, knowing that the past few months had been the happiest of his entire life.

They had been married in a simple, civil service held at the local registrar's office in London before she'd flown back to Mallorca with him. It was what they had both wanted so there had been no reason to wait. Now he pulled her into his arms and gave her a gentle kiss before handing her the letter that had arrived from London.

They had made a formal application to adopt Josh before leaving England. He knew that Rebecca had been terrified that Tara might lodge an objection once their solicitor informed her of their plans, but it hadn't happened. Now he smiled when he heard her gasp of relief as she read the letter.

'See, it is official now. We are legally Josh's parents.'

'I kept wondering if something would go wrong at the last minute,' she admitted with a catch in her voice.

'I know. And it has almost broken my heart, watching you worrying yourself to death.'

He kissed her again, feeling her relax against him as he held her close. 'Everyone knew that it was the best thing for Josh and I had no doubts that it would be perfectly fine in the end. The fact that Tara never bothered to fly back from New York for the hearing proved that she isn't interested in him.'

'I believe she has a new man in her life—a millionaire, so rumour has it.'

'Then she has got what she wanted at last—money,' he said firmly. 'Now we shall forget about her and start to make plans for our future.'

'What have you got in mind?' she asked curiously, tipping back her head to look at him.

'What I have in mind at this minute will have to wait,' he said drily. 'I am needed at the clinic. My colleagues are already talking about the amount of time I have taken off recently.'

'Let them talk,' she murmured, kissing his jaw and smiling when she felt his body immediately quicken.

'Mmm, you can be so very persuasive, Rebecca...' He kissed her quickly then set her away from him and sighed. 'No, I must not be tempted. There is something I want to ask you first.'

'That sounds very serious,' she teased, smiling up at him with her heart in her eyes.

Felipe smiled back. 'It is something I have been thinking about for some time, but I thought it might be better to wait until everything had been finalised. Now we shall be able to have a double celebration.'

Becky shook her head. 'I'm not sure I understand.'

'It is simple, *querida*.' He took her hands and held them tightly as he looked into her eyes. 'I have spoken to the priest at our local church and he has agreed to bless our marriage, if you like the idea.'

'Oh, I do!' She laughed in delight. 'I can't think of anything I would like more, in fact!'

'Good. I also thought that it might be nice to have a party here at the villa to celebrate after the service.' He bent and kissed her lightly on the mouth. 'We can also celebrate the fact that Josh is ours and that nobody can ever take him away from us.'

'That would be wonderful, Felipe.'

She bent and lifted Josh into her arms as he came toddling into the study to find them. There was a light in her eyes when she looked at him that made Felipe's breath catch. 'I can't think of anything I want more than to let everyone share our happiness.'

'Neither can I,' he said deeply. He bent and kissed her, laughing when Josh pushed between them and held up his face to be kissed as well. They both kissed him then Rebecca put him down when he started wriggling.

Felipe put his arms around her as they watched him making a beeline for the desk. There were tears in Felipe's eyes but he didn't try to hide them from her. 'Antonio would be so glad to know that his son was loved like this, Rebecca.'

'He would, and I think he would be glad for us, too.' She turned to face him. 'I love you, Felipe.'

'And I love you, too.'

He kissed her hungrily, held her to his heart and knew that he had never felt more blessed.

He had Rebecca.

He had his brother's son.

He couldn't have wished for anything else!

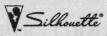

SPECIAL EDITION™

Discover why readers love Sherryl Woods!

THE ROSE COTTAGE SISTERS

Love and laughter surprise them at their childhood haven.

For the Love of Pete
by

SHERRYL WOODS

Jo D'Angelo's sisters knew what she needed—a retreat to Rose Cottage to grieve her broken engagement. And their plan was working—until Jo came face-to-face with the first man ever to break her heart, Pete Catlett, who had ended their idyllic summer love affair when he got another girl pregnant. Pete vowed to gain Jo's forgiveness for his betrayal...and perhaps win her back in the process.

Silhouette Special Edition #1687
On sale June 2005!

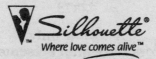

Where love comes alive™

Introducing a brand-new trilogy by

Sharon Kendrick

**Passion, power and privilege—the dynasty
continues with these handsome princes...**

THE
ROYAL HOUSE
OF
CACCIATORE

Welcome to Mardivino—a beautiful and
wealthy Mediterranean island principality,
with a prestigious and glamorous royal family.
There are three Cacciatore princes—Nicolo,
Guido and the eldest, the heir, Gianferro.

This month (May 2005) you can meet Nico in
THE MEDITERRANEAN
PRINCE'S PASSION #2466

Next month (June 2005) read Guido's story in
THE PRINCE'S LOVE-CHILD #2472

Coming in July: Gianferro's story in
THE FUTURE KING'S BRIDE #2478

HARLEQUIN®
Presents

Seduction and Passion Guaranteed!

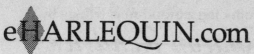

SPOTLIGHT

**A NEW 12-book series featuring
the reader-favorite Fortune family
launches in June 2005!**

THE
F⊙RTUNES
OF TEXAS:
Reunion

Cowboy at Midnight

by *USA TODAY* bestselling author

ANN MAJOR

Rancher Steven Fortune considered
himself lucky. He had a successful
ranch, good looks and many female
companions. But when the contented
bachelor meets events planner
Amy Burke-Sinclair, he finds
himself bitten by the love bug!

**The Fortunes of Texas:
Reunion—**
The power of family.

Exclusive Extras!
Family Tree...
Character Profiles...
Sneak Peek

Silhouette®
Where love comes alive™

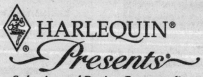